THE BEAST MUST DIE

THE BEAST ARISES

Discover the latest books in this multi-volume series at
blacklibrary.com

THE BEAST ARISES

BOOK EIGHT

THE BEAST MUST DIE

GAV THORPE

BLACK LIBRARY

For the original and still best Grand Warlord – Adrian Wood. Waaagh!

A BLACK LIBRARY PUBLICATION

First published in Great Britain in 2016 by
Black Library
Games Workshop Ltd
Willow Road
Nottingham NG7 2WS UK

10 9 8 7 6 5 4 3 2 1

Cover art by Víctor Manuel Leza Moreno.

A CIP record for this book is available from the British Library.

UK ISBN 13: 978 1 78496 199 2
US ISBN 13: 978 1 78496 200 5

See Black Library on the internet at

blacklibrary.com

Find out more about Games Workshop
and the world of Warhammer 40,000 at

games-workshop.com

Printed and bound in China

Fire sputters...
The shame of our deaths
and our heresies is done. They are
behind us, like wretched phantoms. This
is a new age, a strong age, an age of Imperium.
Despite our losses, despite the fallen sons, despite the
eternal silence of the Emperor, now watching over us in
spirit instead of in person, we will endure. There will be no
more war on such a perilous scale. There will be an end
to wanton destruction. Yes, foes will come and
enemies will arise. Our security will be
threatened, but we will be ready, our
mighty fists raised. There will be no
great war to challenge us now.
We will not be brought
to the brink like that
again...

'In my long years I have found that if one stares too long into the eye of the Beast, the Beast not only stares back but takes the opportunity to bite off your face. Decisive action – any action – far outweighs excessive contemplation.'

Attr. Leman Russ (unverified)

CHAPTER ONE

Terra – the Imperial Palace

We fell and we burned. Not just one, but all. These are the ashes we are left. The splinters of broken glass left of the window through which we watched humanity die. This is not our world, but they are not strong enough. Why? What was His plan? A crumbling ruin, a cruel joke. The blood in the veins is weak. But it is blood and it will bleed. It needs to bleed. To cleanse the infection. Purgation. Pain. Nothing is achieved without sacrifice.

Was that His plan all along?

The Senatorum Imperialis had long been a circus in the eyes of Grand Master Vangorich, but of late its habit of convening meetings in different locations had turned it into a travelling show. Security, his fellow High Lords had insisted. With an ork attack moon still lurking within striking distance, albeit silenced and blockaded for the moment, it was unwise to meet in the same location on successive occasions.

He was unsure how it was more secure or morale-boosting to meet beneath the cracked dome of the Anesidoran

Chapel – once such a proud statement of Imperial Faith and power – when the chapel's mosaics and friezes bore the scars from the attack moon's arrival.

Most of the elaborate decorum of the High Lords' conclaves had been gradually stripped away by each episode in the growing tragedy enveloping Terra and the Segmentum Solar. Gone were the hordes of retainers, the pomp of the Lucifer Blacks in escort, the self-important clarions and gaily coloured banners.

The entourage of clerks, administrators, vox- and vid-datacordists, factotums and counsellors was much diminished, replaced in part by two companies of Lucifer Blacks in combat gear rather than ceremonial uniforms. It made the large, echoing space of the chapel's nave seem even grander, even emptier without the attendant background noise of teeming functionaries that had used to fill it with their tapping, scribbling and murmuring.

The Imperial Palace, the whole sprawling edifice, seemed overly grandiose. At least, Vangorich felt it so. The parade grounds built for Legions stood empty. Halls dedicated to the assembly of thousands in audience lay dusty and unused. Vast wings had been erected to house the armies of administrators that had been spawned over the last millennia, while the immensity of the past was allowed to remain standing idle, each vacant shell a hollow claim to a power that had long departed.

The High Lords seemed small and frail surrounded by the vastness of the chapel, as if it represented the scale of the threat they faced. In a palace built for demigods, they seemed more insignificant than ever.

Vangorich moved in the shadows beyond the central meeting, only half-listening to the back and forth of bickering and politics. He measured each man and woman at the table, recalling plans long in motion, schemes that had been devised over many years lest the need arise.

He knew exactly how each would die, if necessary. That was his role, though none subjected to his scrutiny would care to admit as much.

Take Mesring, for example. The Ecclesiarch thought himself safe, having uncovered and possibly countered the toxin Vangorich had introduced into his system. It might be a bluff, might be that the seed of Mesring's destruction still tainted the blood in his veins, but it mattered nothing to the Grand Master if it was not. His agents had poisoned the head of the Imperial Church once, and they could do it again. Next time it would not be for leverage, it would be quick-acting and lethal.

Then Lansung, the Lord High Admiral, saviour and failure in one body. Vangorich often tempted himself with the idea that his own hand would deliver the blow here. Of them all, Lansung's megalomania and vainglory had caused the most damage. But it was not the Grand Master's position to strike the fatal blow. Not always. He was the hand that held the dagger, not the blade itself.

In passing, he caught the eye of his operative amongst the minions hovering close to the High Lords. It was remarkable how so lethal an individual, one so possessed of physical strength and dexterity, could masquerade his puissance beneath the plain green cowl and cape of an Administratum adept, his size and power hidden as easily as the mono-stiletto he carried. The weapon was fashioned from gene-modified bone as hard as steel. Organic matter, invisible to any auspex currently known to the minds of the Adeptus Mechanicus.

Esad Wire, the Beast, Vangorich's right hand during the unfolding catastrophe. The Beast did not react to the brief glance of his master, his attention fixed on the proceedings of the High Lords, features hidden in the darkness beneath his cowl.

And there was Kubik, Fabricator General, head of the Cult Mechanicus. Today he was present only in hololithic representation. Perhaps he feared to attend in person after the revelations of previous gatherings. The Adeptus Mechanicus' long-standing relationship with the Imperium of Terra had been fractious of late. Agendas had clashed, information had been hoarded, loyalties had been called into question.

Vangorich looked at the static-flecked image of the Martian overlord and wondered whether recent protestations of renewed dedication to the Imperial cause were simply more lies. In a show of cooperation, Kubik had shared – under duress – the findings regarding the ork teleporter technology and the location of Ullanor, the world from which this threat seemed to have sprung.

The Grand Master had plans and agents in place within the Adeptus Mechanicus on both Terra and Mars to extract what further information was being hidden and, if ultimate sanction was required, to strike at Kubik himself.

The only other individuals of importance were missing. Veritus and Wienand, the joint Inquisitorial Representatives, had not made any communication since Koorland's return from his mission, and whether by choice or from the ongoing machinations of the Inquisition was not clear. It irritated Vangorich that he was unsure of their current whereabouts, but as he had found, sometimes it was best not to worry too much. Much as with his own organisation, when the Inquisition could be seen at work was when it was too late.

An approaching thunder silenced the discussion and all eyes turned to the great doors of the chapel. The Lucifer Blacks parted swiftly as a handful of commanders from the Adeptus Astartes entered, their armoured boots striking deafening drumbeats across the broken tiles. They were a few individuals, but each was the avatar of a martial power deemed so strong it had been divided, their might judged too much for a single hand to wield. And now that edict was being reversed, and might yet prove a greater threat than the orks.

Space Marines. Each dwarfed the chapel's occupants: just the seven present were capable of killing everyone within, including the Lucifer Blacks. Except Vangorich, of course. At any given heartbeat he knew precisely which of the four escape routes he might use should the Adeptus Astartes decide that pandering to the pride and ambition of these mortals was too much effort.

Captain Valefor of the Blood Angels. Wolf Lord Asger of the Space Wolves. Chapter Master Odaenathus of the Ultramarines and Grand Master Sachael of the Dark Angels, both newly arrived on Terra, fresh come from battles in the darkest reaches of the galaxy. Their Chapters bore the names of the greatest Legions from the Heresy War, and carried that distinction well.

With them came High Marshal Bohemond of the Black Templars and Chapter Master Quesadra of the Crimson Fists. Both had earned glory in the battles against the orks thus far, each creating a legacy worthy of Rogal Dorn from whom their gene-seed had been created. Others were continuing the fight, in the Sol System and beyond.

And with these lords of the Space Marines arrived the last of Dorn's sons, the remaining survivor of the Imperial Fists. Captain, Chapter Master and, lately, Lord Commander Koorland, who had resumed the use of his wall-name, Slaughter. His ochre plate had recently been repaired and repainted, but the injury of war and loss was borne in his eyes. Dark, distant, they looked upon the High Lords as though surveying pieces of furniture. A necessary but uninteresting feature of the environment.

And then came Vulkan, and suddenly the mighty halls, kilometres-long processionals and cavernous chapel did not seem so large after all.

The primarch filled the huge space, and not just with his gigantic physique; the raw presence of the Emperor's warlord was like a force that swept all before it. A few of the High Lords stood up on reflex, some bowed, and all but Vangorich averted their gaze, however briefly.

His armour, plate worthy of a demigod and forged by his own hand, was burnished dark green and gold. In one fist he bore a hammer the size of a Lucifer Black and many times more deadly. His skin was ebon, as dark as a starless night, save for two eyes that glittered like rubies.

They found Vangorich immediately despite his attempts at being inconspicuous, effortlessly identifying and locating the greatest potential threat in the chapel. He flinched at their silent interrogation, his unfettered reaction providing the answer they sought. A hint of a smile creased the primarch's lips for half a heartbeat. A challenge, almost.

He knew.

Vulkan knew Vangorich had a plan to kill even a primarch. The Grand Master had to, it was the inevitable logic of his position. Duty compelled him to consider such a terrible scenario.

Vulkan's eyes moved on, releasing Vangorich from their burning intensity, the primarch's expression sour as he took in the surroundings and the holy nature of their decoration. The giant turned his gaze back to the others. However, his next words were directed towards the Master of Assassins.

'Grand Master Vangorich, what is our purpose in going to Ullanor?'

'You ask me because I am the Assassin, lord primarch, which gives us our answer,' the Grand Master replied smoothly, moving into the light, drawn forth like venom from a bite. 'To slay the Great Beast. We know that orks follow the strongest leader. Take that away and they will fall on each other in the resulting power vacuum. The invasion will splinter and die. For all their barbaric strength, they are vulnerable to a classic decapitation strike.'

'Had we known that Ullanor was the source, I would have directed efforts thus,' protested Lansung. He wilted a little as Vulkan's unforgiving gaze moved to him, but retained enough composure to redirect the primarch's ire. 'Had the Fabricator General not withheld such intelligence, we might have ended this sooner.'

Even across the medium of the hololithic transmitter, Kubik looked unsettled.

Vulkan said nothing, but moved to one end of the debating table as his commanders spread to either side. Vangorich tried not to think of it as an encircling manoeuvre, but he quickly reassessed his options and concluded that only two escape routes remained.

'The full weight of Mars is being directed to support the assault of the lord primarch,' Kubik's voice buzzed from a vox-caster placed in front of his hazy image, 'as swiftly as it can be mustered. Dominus Gerg Zhokuv is one of our best and most experienced commanders from the Taghmata.'

'One of your best?' said Vulkan.

'*The* best!' Kubik quickly answered. 'His logistaria and strategic engrams date back to the Heresy War and earlier.'

'The ships are ready?' Vulkan demanded of Lansung.

The Lord High Admiral nodded without comment.

'I have put out the call for the Frateris to assemble. Thousands of followers are ready to embark as soon...' Mesring trailed off in the face of Vulkan's unflinching stare.

'That will not be necessary, *Ecclesiarch*.' The primarch's distaste for Mesring's position made the title sound like a curse. 'Your brand of zealotry will not serve our cause.'

Vangorich was so busy enjoying Mesring's utter despondency that he almost missed a small reaction from Bohemond. The High Marshal glanced sideways at the primarch, and then fixed his gaze on a point on the ground for several heartbeats. Nobody else seemed to notice and Vangorich wondered what could prompt such a guilt reflex.

Tobris Ekharth, Master of the Administratum, cleared his

throat. His eyes momentarily flicked from one High Lord to the next, seeking reassurance and receiving little, until they rested again on the sheaf of translucent datasheets in his quivering hands. He swallowed hard.

'I... That is, my organisation...' He sniffed, gripped his reports tighter and started again. The words burst forth in a breathless stream. 'This whole process is without mandate or proper protocols, and is not in compliance with at least seventy-two per cent of the Senatorum Imperialis code, not least being the exclusion of required officials to make proper record and deliver due notification on the deliberations and ramifications of gatherings at which Imperial policy and the application of military resource of greater than regiment-strength or equivalent thereof has been debated.'

'I am quite sure that half of those words were not in the correct order,' said Odaenathus. 'Are you objecting to something?'

'This war,' Ekharth blurted, 'is illegal! Without proper authority. Of uncertain integrity.' The next word was uttered with such contempt that it made Vangorich wince. 'Unauthorised...'

'You mentioned compliance,' said Vulkan, folding his arms. 'That word can mean many things. In one respect, it is something with which I am more familiar than any other in this chamber.'

'I don't understand,' confessed Ekharth, looking to his companion High Lords for support or guidance.

Vangorich laughed gently and he felt their scrutiny and their antipathy. The Master of the Administratum glared at him.

'What is so funny?' Ekharth demanded.

'You seek compliance, my dear Tobris.' Vangorich looked across to Vulkan. 'Worlds brought into the Imperial Truth during the Great Crusade were "compliant". The lord primarch has several thousand Space Marines poised at his command, in orbit and on the surface of Terra. It is we that need to consider the nature of compliance.'

Silence followed for several seconds. Vulkan did not gainsay Vangorich's assertion.

'Good.' The primarch nodded. 'We are of one mind. Let us turn our efforts to Ullanor and the matter at hand. Now the war truly begins.'

CHAPTER TWO

Ullanor – outer system

Peace is deception. It does not last. It cannot last. The enemy is always waiting. The fight is endless, relentless. A tide that rises. Even when it recedes it takes away. It erodes. Nagging, gnawing, grinding. Slowly, war after war, battle after battle, fight after fight, every grain dropping away, washed into nothingness. Peace is the breath between shouts. The inhalation before the gasp of pain or ecstasy. Why can we not forge peace? Forges make weapons. Only war, merciless and constant, is truth.

The Adeptus Astartes were in the vanguard.

As always.

Rapid strike vessels, cruisers and battle-barges pierced the Ullanor system, a slashing sabre to open up the orks' defences and leave the xenos unable to counter the more ponderous but powerful blows of the Imperial Navy, Adeptus Mechanicus and Astra Militarum.

Guided by the most able Navigators of the Navis Nobilite,

the ships of the Space Marines convened within days of each other, despite the usual vagaries of the warp and the ever-present ork psychic disturbance that had come to be known as the green roar. Auspex arrays scoured the system for all signs of the enemy. Weapon decks and gun turrets were poised to unleash incredible firepower. The vessels of the Space Marines pushed hard from their translation points around the perimeter of the Ullanor system.

The outer system was an anarchic tempest of asteroids, lost moons, nebulous vapour clouds and wayward comets, thrown into terrible storms by the orbits of three super gas giants. Within this navigational horror lurked relative normality. There were eight more planets, three of them lethal gas worlds, though three inner micro-planets and a frozen Terra-sized globe showed signs of low level habitation. The fourth out from the red star was the only major populated sphere – Ullanor Prime.

There were also orks. Many, many orks.

The Ullanor system was awash with starships, an armada of vessels coursing to or from the ork world in the inner system. Ships of all descriptions plied the routes from the safe translation zone far from Ullanor's star. Alien-built freighters with ramshackle hulls encased in shimmering fields moved alongside stolen cargo haulers with sputtering void shields, bearing the insignia of Imperial merchant houses defaced by orkish glyphs. A score of warships lost against the green menace had been taken, their crippled hulls pressed into service as bulk carriers: flight decks and gun bays stripped, the weapons stolen to bolster the armaments of the escorts.

The *Reprisal* was the first to lie alongside one of these. A force of Dark Angels Terminators teleported across, led by Grand Master Sachael.

The heavily armoured elite of the Deathwing company faced nothing more threatening than a few dozen orks – brutish overseers that had enslaved the crew of the ship, no match for the First Company of the Dark Angels. Searching through the ship for any surviving foes, Sachael was disgusted by what they found.

The orks had shown little regard for their captives, content to give them the bare minimum of food, water and heat. The air was freezing, the rag-clad slaves close to exhaustion and death from exposure. Many hundreds had not survived, their bodies left where they had fallen, some cleared away into the disused ammunition magazines and food storage halls. Vermin and insects were everywhere, fungal growths from ork spores lying in a patina across metal bulkheads and plasteel decking.

Interviewing the captives revealed that the vessel had been overrun when the orks had invaded the Trolgeth System. Nobody knew the fate of the freshly raised regiment of several thousand soldiers *IG-8112* had been carrying, except that they had been taken from the ship on ork transports in orbit over Ullanor. Since then the vessel had been making supply runs, though to and from which systems and with what cargo the battered crew remained ignorant of.

'They drove us, saviour, drove us something wicked,' one emaciated soul told the Grand Master, emerging from the darkness of a sub-hold, blinking in the lamplight from Sachael's Tactical Dreadnought armour. His pallid skin was

broken by sores and whip marks, bruised and grazed along the spine and shoulders where he had carried heavy loads. 'Killed the officers first. Ate them, right in front of us. Raw and bloody, it was.'

'They came for us, they came for us!' squealed another unfortunate. He fell to the floor at the Grand Master's feet, pawing at the armoured boots, drooling and wild-eyed. 'They came for us!'

Two more moved forward and dragged him back, flinching as if expecting blows to rain down on them.

'No Geller fields, saviour, you see?' explained the first man. 'They got a shield, of a sort. It softens the voices, dulls the dreams. But it don't take them away. Not proper. Three trips we made, away and back and away again. Six journeys through the warp. More killed 'emselves than died from lack of nourishment, I reckon. Or killed others... We had to... They needed stopping.'

His gaze was haunted and he glanced down at his dirty hands. Sachael understood the meaning.

'You gave them the Emperor's mercy and saved the lives of your companions. There is no shame in that.'

'Emperor defend us, that's the truth,' said another of the internees.

'Is we safe?' A woman draped in the remains of an old grain sack tottered out from the crowd. 'Is we safe yet?'

'More ships are coming,' Sachael assured them. 'The Imperial Navy. They'll send over new officers to take you away from here.'

'Emperor bless the Navy,' she cried, tears welling up in her eyes. She blinked forcefully and fell to her knees, hands clasped in prayer. 'And gratitude to the Emperor for send-ing His Space Marines to deliver us from evil. Great is His benevolence.'

'Praise Him,' others chorused, entwining their thumbs and splaying their palms across their chests in a crude approximation of the eagle of the Imperial aquila.

'Angels of mercy!'

'Divine guardians!'

'Praise the Dark Angels!'

Sachael backed away, uncomfortable with their adora-tion. His second, Sergeant Gadariel, approached, the bulk of his Terminator armour barely fitting through the door in the bulkhead.

'No more xenos, Grand Master,' he reported over the vox. 'Main hold is filled with perishable food. Thousands of tonnes. Shall we let these poor wretches have some?'

'Not yet,' Sachael replied, turning away from the freed slaves. 'They need proper rehabilitation and we do not have time nor means for such measures. Lock the holds.'

'They are starving, Grand Master.'

'And they will have to starve for a few days longer until the Navy arrives and can post armsmen at the holds to stop them killing each other over the food.' Sachael stepped out of the chamber, sparing no glance for the unfortunates. 'We can brook no delays. Our greatest efforts must be spent con-fronting the orks.'

Such experience was repeated on many other ships boarded by the first wave of Space Marines. Like a flock scat-tering before wolves, the ork supply convoys split into the void as the Adeptus Astartes continued their encroachment and more Imperial ships broke warp at the system boundary. Ship commanders were caught between the need to press in-system and secure passage towards their target, and their desire to board or destroy as many of the captured vessels as they could.

The faster vessels, rapid strike craft crewed by a few Space Marines, darted across the vacuum hunting down such ships as could be easily overhauled. On many of these ships the appearance of the Space Marines, even just a handful, was enough to rouse the crews from their timidity, and they used chains, tools and bare hands to fight back against their greenskin enslavers. Thousands died in these shipborne uprisings, but many more were freed from nightmarish servitude – and those that gave their lives were considered more fortunate than those that remained on the ships that eluded the pursuit of the Space Marines.

Such actions were admirable, but with each passing hour the penetrating blow of the Space Marine attack dissipated. Flotillas became separated and escorts drawn away from their battle-barges. Ever used to independent action, the captains and masters of the Adeptus Astartes were always ready to act on their own initiative.

From aboard the *Alcazar Remembered,* Koorland observed this dissolution of force with some unease. Leaving Thane with orders to continue on as fast as possible, Koorland left the command bridge and descended to the armoury bay that had been rapidly reconfigured into quarters for Vulkan.

The twin sliding doors were open as Koorland approached, allowing the flaring sparks and crackle of a laswelder to pass into the corridor. He stopped at the threshold and looked within.

Vulkan was stooped over a worktable – the heavy bench had been set onto a plinth, but it still barely came up to the primarch's waist. He was stripped down to the inner harness of his war-plate, revealing jet-black skin marked across every square centimetre with scars, tattoos and brand marks. An assortment of armoured plates, stacked crystal cells, cabling and bolts were carefully arranged on the table. Laswelder in one hand, Vulkan lifted a sheet of ceramite and inspected it closely.

'You may enter, Koorland,' said the primarch, not looking up from his work.

'I am Slaughter,' the Imperial Fist replied. 'My wall-name.'

'You are not on the wall now, Son of Dorn.'

'We are the Last Wall, my lord. It is a state of mind, not a geographic location.'

'I know,' said Vulkan, smiling as he placed the ceramite and laswelder on the bench and straightened. 'I was there when Dorn took the first wall-name at the last defence of the Emperor's Palace. Do you remember what it was?'

Koorland stepped into the primarch's chamber, which had not altered much with its change of purpose. Materials and tools lined the walls on hooks and shelves, boxes were stacked neatly beneath them. A table to one side held a few books, data crystals, a scattering of personal effects. Doomtremor lay on the bare metal, glinting beneath the lumen strips. There were no luxuries – if the primarch slept, it was on metal decking.

'Of course, my lord.' Koorland stopped a few metres from the bench. 'Defiance. Lord Dorn took the name Defiance.'

'He did.' The primarch's smile slipped away and his focus shifted, lost in a moment of recollection.

'The fleet is dispersing, my lord. The orks are not fighting. They flee as soon as we approach. Even vessels obviously built as warships are avoiding confrontation if they can. The rapidity of our advance is drawing us away from the Mandeville boundary and only a few of our allies' ships have arrived.'

'And what do you wish to do, Koorland?'

'I am Slaughter, my lord.' He did not know why the primarch insisted on using his other name, but he had to assume it was not for insult. Perhaps he was trying to make some point that the Imperial Fist did not understand. 'We need to issue orders to consolidate our positions before we push again for Ullanor orbit.'

'A reasonable plan. Why have you not yet implemented it?'

'I...' Koorland frowned. 'You are the primarch, my lord. The fleet, the warriors, they fight under your command.'

'And I give you my full authority,' said Vulkan. He lifted up a jar of lubricant and dipped a finger into it, the digit barely fitting. He started to apply the unguent to a metal coil. 'You have commanded planetary landings before, Koorland. You do not need me looking over your shoulder.'

'I would prefer... My lord, the High Lords have entrusted this expedition to us on the belief that you will command it. I have led Space Marines, but we also have Adeptus Mechanicus, Imperial Navy and Astra Militarum forces here too. Only a primarch, only *you* have experience leading such an armada.'

Vulkan stopped his work and drew in a breath, laying

his hands flat on the table as though steadying himself, though more likely steadying his thoughts. By the accounts from Thane, Vulkan's battle-wrath was every bit as mighty as the legends portrayed but here he was patience personified.

'The last time warriors of the Emperor attacked this world, the force consisted of a hundred thousand Space Marines, eight million soldiers of the Imperial Army, a legion of a hundred Titans and over six hundred warships to protect the thousands of transports to carry them.' Vulkan wiped his hands on a rag of cloth large enough to be a serviceable battle standard. 'You have to worry about roughly a tenth of that.'

Koorland nodded, accepting the subtle chastisement, although he was still not comfortable with the task Vulkan handed him. The primarch read the reluctance in his expression.

'That armada was led by a primarch. His name was Horus. The victory earned him the title of Warmaster.' Vulkan's shoulders tensed as he turned back to the work bench. He toyed with a few items, his hands deft despite their size. 'We both know how that ended, Koorland.'

'I am Slaughter.' The reply was an unthinking instinct, but Vulkan snapped his gaze onto the Space Marine, brow furrowed with displeasure.

'You are *Lord Commander Koorland*,' growled the primarch. 'You took that title freely. Now it is time to live up to it.'

Koorland stepped back, physically reeling from the rebuke as if struck. Recovering, he bowed to Vulkan, ashamed that he had disappointed the primarch. Vulkan's disapproval was more injurious than any physical wound the Imperial Fist had suffered, the thought of it nearly as painful as the memory of Ardamantua. Swallowing hard, he resolved never to feel such disgrace again.

'As you will it, Lord Vulkan. In your name, for the memory of Defiance and of the Lord Guilliman who first held the title, I shall continue as Lord Commander.'

Vulkan gave him a nod, a quick gesture but one that sent a surge of strength through Koorland. As easily as the primarch's disapproval had dashed him down, his simple endorsement gave the Lord Commander renewed confidence and hope.

It was not until he was halfway back to the command bridge that he reflected on Vulkan's words. To take Ullanor, Horus himself had commanded ten times the force at Koorland's disposal. Koorland's new optimism fled like sunlight at dusk.

CHAPTER THREE

The overture has begun. A while remains until the main movement begins.

Time is the enemy of peace, peace the enemy of sanity. I do not need to ponder, I have many lifetimes of sorrows to occupy me. Let us be at the matter and bring it to swift resolution.

But it is not your place any more. That was the disaster. Even before the corruption, we were poor lords. No leader save He alone should be greater than his followers. He must value them more than they value him.

Why did we not understand that before?

Melta charges turned the airlock door into slag in milliseconds, filling the corridor beyond with vapour and fiery particles. Valefor of the Blood Angels was the first through the breach, molten armaplas flecking his red armour as he pushed through the haze.

Bullets whined down the corridor and ricocheted from his

war-plate while las-beams seared narrow welts across the ceramite. He lifted his pistol to reply with equal force, only for his finger to remain still – his attackers were not orks.

The volley of fire spewed towards him came from the pistols and rifles of human crew. A shotgun blazed as an armsman opened fire, spattering the Blood Angels captain with pellets.

'Hold your fire!' he bellowed, levelling his sword at the five Sanguinary Guard of his retinue that followed from the assault pod. Another flurry of bullets rattled around him and he returned his attention to the men in front. 'Stop shooting, in the Emperor's name!'

His words fell on deaf ears. Valefor's auto-senses adjusted as the glare of entry faded, revealing more details of his attackers. They wore patched uniforms, some of them little more than rags held together by crude stitching and maintenance tape. Ork glyphs had been painted onto the fabric and the crew members wore necklaces of human teeth. Their cheeks and brows bore scars and other tribal markings.

'Cleanse the traitors,' spat the captain, opening fire. His shots cut through the nearest trio, spattering the bulkheads with their blood. More bolts flared past as the Sanguinary Guard unleashed their Angelus bolters, turning another dozen foes to broken flesh.

Valefor launched himself into the remaining crew, his power sword a golden shaft of light in his fist. He parted limbs and bodies with every slash and thrust, the continuing storm of fire from his companions tearing around him.

In a few more seconds they had reached an arterial

corridor, emerging into a fresh conflagration of fire from all directions. On galleries above and through open doors, the crew of the boarded ship spilled forth like ants from their nest. Their calls were more like the grunting of animals, low and hoarse. The walls were clumsily painted with more ork glyphmarks, and piles of filth littered the deck. Chains and cables strung with bones and hunks of scrap metal hung from gallery to gallery in rough ornamentation.

The crew were savage, hollering and hooting as they poured along balconies and through the corridors, brandishing their weapons, firing wildly at the interlopers.

'Orks in human bodies,' muttered Sergeant Marbas. The veteran levelled his wrist-mounted bolter and sent a salvo of shots slashing through the closest crew.

'This ship was not overrun in these past months of invasion,' replied Valefor, adding his own bolts to the furious storm cutting along the corridor from his Sanguinary Guard. 'These wretches have long been under the dominance of the greenskins.'

Marbas growled. 'Did none stand guard for these lost worlds? Did none count their fall?'

'I am sure reports of their loss lie somewhere on the desk of an Administratum clerk, unseen beneath tithe receipts and Astra Militarum levy charters,' said Valefor. 'We cannot be absolved of blame. We are the defenders of humanity – it is our watch that also fell lax.'

'We cannot be everywhere, captain. How are we to safeguard a million worlds if they do not call for our aid?'

The crew withdrew a distance, cowed by the firepower of the Space Marines, their laspistols and shotguns of little use against Adeptus Astartes battleplate, their aim as woeful as the xenos that dominated them. The savages jeered and screeched, baring their teeth as if they had tusks and fangs like their ork masters.

Amongst the raucous cries and shouts, Valefor heard an undercurrent of another sound, a repetitive noise that grew in volume, taking over the disparate bellows and snarls. Through the roar of bolters, snap of lasguns and the shouts of the wounded and dying, he recognised a single word over and over, a guttural chant in crude Low Gothic.

'Beast! Beast! Beast! Beast!' The war chant echoed through the ship, accompanied by pounding fists and stamping feet, causing the entire corridor to reverberate.

'They are lost to the Emperor,' said Marbas. 'They serve another, more immediate power.'

'There is nothing to be salvaged here,' snarled Valefor, withdrawing back into the accessway, moving out of the welter of las-blasts and projectiles.

The Sanguinary Guard followed, stepping backwards as they continued their volleys of bolts. A woman emerged from a hatch to their right, barking madly as she threw herself at Valefor, daggers improvised out of plasteel sheets in her fists. She wore daubs of black face paint, and a headscarf checked in black and white – a pattern Valefor had seen on many an ork banner. The tip of his sword found her throat even as she scrambled to her feet, snarling becoming a death rattle as she folded to the deck. Others were pushing through the maintenance shaft after her. Valefor kicked the first back into the tunnel and tossed a frag grenade into the open hatch. He stepped back as the detonation filled the small space with deadly shrapnel, then signalled to his vessel.

'*Sanguinem Ignis*. We are ceasing the boarding action. When we are clear, turn this ship to plasma.'

Thane turned at the sound of the command bridge doors opening. He caught his breath as Vulkan ducked beneath the lintel. Fully armoured, he was as big as a Dreadnought and the battle-barge's bridge, though large by human standards, seemed barely able to contain his presence. The Chapter Master of the Fists Exemplar stepped to one side as Vulkan took the centre of the chamber.

Others turned at their stations – those capable of independent thought did. Thane saw veterans of dozens of battles trembling in the presence of the Emperor's son. Several unaugmented crew muttered invocations and bowed their heads.

Thane let out a breath he hadn't realised he had been holding.

It was the primarch's first appearance on the command deck since he had come aboard. His presence lightened Thane's mood, reassuring and strong in equal measure. Koorland followed a few steps behind, his expression guarded.

'Welcome to the *Alcazar Remembered*, lord primarch. I am sorry I did not get to extend a greeting on your arrival.'

Vulkan said nothing and eyed the main display.

'A Salamanders strike cruiser arrived in-system yesterday, my lord,' Thane continued. 'They requested an audience.'

'No,' Vulkan replied, still examining the scanner feeds. 'They will operate as part of the force without favour. Seeing me will only... distract them.'

'They will be disappointed.'

'That is all?' the primarch said, turning to Thane. 'A few battle stations and a handful of warships?'

'We can detect no other orbital defences, lord primarch.'

Koorland stepped forward. 'I have sent Chapter Master Odaenathus and High Marshal Bohemond to lead the attacks against the orbital platforms. Admiral Villiers and the survivors of the Third Coreward Flotilla are clearing out the remaining starships while Admiral Acharya creates a high orbital blockade.' He took a breath and his gaze moved between the primarch and the screen and back again. 'Within ten hours we will have full orbital supremacy.'

'I see.' Vulkan placed his hands together, palm to palm, resting against his plastron as if in prayer. He did not look pleased. 'Are we to truly believe that we have seized Ullanor, homeworld of the Beast that has unleashed untold destruction across the Segmentum Solar, within ten days of arrival, and with the loss of only two frigates, one destroyer and less than twenty Space Marines?'

'That is the situation at present, lord primarch,' said Thane.

Vulkan accepted this in silence, looking at Koorland expectantly. The Lord Commander ground his teeth in thought for a short time.

'We cannot dispute the facts as they are,' he said slowly, considering his words. 'Orbital dominance is assured and the ork fleet is scattered. The Imperial Navy is capable of creating an outer blockade against any counter-attack. The next phase must be surface assault. We need a war council to decide the strategy and plan of attack.'

'Very well,' Vulkan said with a nod. 'By my authority, make it so.'

The primarch left, and with his departure the bridge regained something of its old dimensions, the background mood losing some of its intensity. Thane approached Koorland.

'Why does he not issue the command himself?' the Exemplar asked. 'He seems... disinterested in the entire endeavour.'

Koorland laid a hand on Thane's pauldron.

'He is a primarch, a son of the Emperor. I do not try to guess his thoughts, but I have no doubt of his motivations. He has brought us here to kill the Great Beast, and that is what we shall do.'

'Then I will share your confidence, brother,' said Thane. 'Who shall we bring to the war council?'

'All of them,' replied the Lord Commander. 'Chapter Masters and command-level captains, admirals and commodores, and don't forget Dominus Gerg Zhokuv and whichever subordinates he wishes to bring.'

'And what is to be the strategy, brother?'

'We find the Great Beast, attack with everything we have, and destroy it.'

The words were simple enough, but the look Koorland exchanged with Thane confirmed the Exemplar's belief that the execution, literal and figurative, would be far from straightforward.

The lexmechanic's voicebox had an irritating static interference that made her sibilants sound like a hissing snake. Koorland tried to ignore the aural tic so that he could concentrate on the tech-priest's analysis. She was currently pointing with a reticulated mechanical limb at a greyish globe dominating the hololith display that hung in the middle of the briefing chamber.

The room was dark, illuminated only by the sparse light coming from the projector. The gloom did nothing to alleviate the claustrophobic conditions of a chamber built for half a dozen officers filled with twice that number and their attendants, not to mention the dominating presence of Vulkan looming over them all from beside a blinking bank of strategic cogitators. The primarch had his fingers entwined, his gaze directed off to one side, barely observing the proceedings. Removing the large brushed-steel table had not made much difference, but Koorland was glad of the little extra space that this had afforded.

He shifted his weight, agitated, aware that many of his companions were barely restraining their desire for more determined conversation, only for the sake of appearances observing the niceties of the technical reports and standard liaison protocols. Everyone had something to say but nobody was saying anything yet.

'Electromagnetic dissturbance in the upper ionossphere hasss led to much reflective patterning on our initial orbital ssscan data.' At an unseen command, areas of the slowly spinning globe highlighted in orange, with trails of yellow criss-crossing sections of the remaining whited-out sphere. 'Much of thisss interference can be traced to massive orbital intrusssions. The ressst we expect isss generated by unssshielded industrial ssstructuresss on the sssurface of the planet.'

'Orbital intrusions?' The question was asked by Field-Legatus Otho Dorr, strategic commander of the gathered Astra Militarum forces. In terms of raw manpower, when the remainder of the transports completed the journey into orbit he would lead the largest force – nearly ninety thousand soldiers and ten thousand battle tanks and other vehicles.

'Ship descents and ascents,' explained another of the Cult Mechanicus adherents. He looked much like a crab perched on a hunched human body, a splay of hydraulic appendages like a ruff around his neck. 'Poorly-shielded plasma drives in low orbit, wakes from dirty atomic propellants on shuttlecraft. That sort of thing.'

'A lot of them,' added the dominus.

Koorland knew that it was crude to think of martial prowess in purely physical terms. In fact, to equate pure size with military ability was ork-thought. Yet despite being logically aware of this deficiency in his judgement, he could not help but think of the leader of the Adeptus Mechanicus battle congregation as being somewhat underwhelming.

The dominus was, for the moment, a brain in a glass vessel. An armoured vessel, Koorland conceded, as Gerg Zhokuv continued his detailed explanation of the vacillations and weaknesses of starship augur arrays. Clusters of sensory nodes and rods were mechanical replacements for eyes, nose, ears and skin, linked through spiralling cables attached to sockets in the exterior of the metre-high vessel that two lumbering natal-tank Praetorians had brought to the council room. The biotic fluid inside obscured all but the dark shadow of the organ within, but occasionally Koorland could see there were rods penetrating the naked brain matter. The brain itself was distended, patched in places with inorganic plates, far larger than any normal human skull could contain.

Most disconcerting was that the dominus' 'voice' actually came from the young, waxen-faced man beside the stand on which the pteknopic vessel was set. By some invisible pathway Gerg Zhokuv controlled the slack-faced servitor's body – at least the jaw and vocal cords, for all other facial functions seemed inoperative.

'Can you find it?' Bohemond's growl cut across the dominus' lecture. 'Where is the Great Beast of Ullanor?'

'We have identified several potential locations, hotspots of multi-frequency activity.' There was a pause while Zhokuv's attendants manipulated the display, which flickered with runic lingua-technis inscriptions over several broad zones of red.

'Each of those must be several thousand square kilometres,' said Wolf Lord Asger. 'And there are four of them. That's a quarter of the planet's surface.'

'We need to do better.' Koorland spoke, sensing growing unease between the Space Marines and Adeptus Mechanicus representatives. 'We cannot attack the entire world. We are here to kill the Great Beast, not conquer Ullanor. That is a war for another time. Terra itself is threatened. Time is a luxury.'

His announcement was met with silence for several seconds. Adnachiel, a Company Master from the Dark Angels, spoke next. He pulled back the cowl of his robe and revealed a deeply lined face, grey hair cropped short. Red light glittered in one eye, the lifelike orb hiding a bionic within.

'As nobody else seems willing to raise the point, let me

ask the question that is doubtless on all of our minds.' As he spoke he looked at Vulkan, but his gaze moved to Koorland when he received no response from the primarch. 'Why is Ullanor so poorly defended?'

The obvious answer went unspoken for a few seconds before Bohemond offered an alternative.

'We have seen little strategy in the orks' movements.' He shifted his weight, his black armour reflecting the yellow and green lights from the hololith projector. 'Orks do not consider grander plans, they simply attack until victorious or defeated. I am not surprised that there has been no thought given to the defence of their world.'

'That might be true,' said Asger, 'but for the recent example of the attack moon. I have seen the reports. The orks on the station above Terra lured in the assault, feigning weakness before striking.'

'Had that attack been led by experienced commanders they would have foreseen the danger,' said Bohemond.

'And here we are,' replied Asger.

'So, it's a trap,' said Thane. He looked at the assembled officers and commanders, hoping one might offer an alternative. None of them argued, not even Bohemond.

'A trap we cannot avoid,' said Koorland, his expression sour. 'Perhaps that is the intent. We cannot destroy the Great Beast without landing forces. If we are not here to kill it, we should simply return to Terra and reconsider our options.'

'There will be no withdrawal,' growled Vulkan. He moved into the light of the hololith, filling the room, drawing all eyes. 'The Great Beast dies, or we do. This is how it will be. This is how it *should* be.'

'What do you mean, Lord Vulkan?' asked Zhokuv. 'Point-less expenditure of resources must be avoided. What is to be attained by placing ourselves between the jaws of the enemy if we have no guarantee of success?'

'You wage war with formulae and calculations, magos dominus,' said Vulkan. He narrowed his eyes and then looked away. 'The balance of expense versus gain, parsed through algorithms and logic engines. All is rendered into probability. I must ask you to go further. To have... faith.'

'My lord?' Bohemond was conflicted, his expression vac-illating between confusion and eagerness. 'Faith in what, Lord Vulkan?'

'Ourselves, perhaps,' the primarch replied. 'In justice. In vengeance, if needs be. If that does not suffice, then you must have faith in me. We can do nothing more than strive for victory, even if we cannot see how we might triumph. Magos, do not take this as insult, but there are matters that exist beyond the predictable and physical. The hearts of warriors and the chances of war are not easily codified.'

'I have never claimed as such, lord primarch,' Zhokuv pro-tested. 'My successes have been built upon adaptation and reaction, the ability to respond to the unknowable when it becomes known.'

'Then we shall have faith in the Adeptus Mechanicus, also,' Vulkan replied with a placating smile.

'Faith will not bring forth the Great Beast,' Zhokuv argued through his vox-servitor. 'Application and endeavour will locate the target.'

'As you say, magos dominus, as you say,' Vulkan conceded.

He looked at Koorland, expecting the Lord Commander to continue.

'Application and endeavour,' echoed Koorland. 'We cannot avoid a planetstrike, so we must expend no concern on that front. There is one goal alone that must drive us. To locate the Great Beast. When that is achieved we will bring such force to bear that whatever the orks think they might do, it shall pale in comparison to our fury.'

There were words and gestures of assent from the gathered council. When the others had dispersed, Thane and Koorland were left with Vulkan. The primarch had withdrawn into himself again and stared silently at the slowly revolving hololith of Ullanor.

'You look troubled, my lord,' said Thane.

Vulkan did not move his gaze, but replied softly.

'Rivers follow their course. Animals follow their runs. Events follow required patterns.' He sighed. 'Certain confrontations are inevitable. Unavoidable consequences were set in motion the moment we chose to come to Ullanor.'

'What consequences, my lord?' asked Koorland.

'None that we can evade, Koorland,' said the primarch. 'But we must prevail or all is lost. As I said, we must all show a little faith.'

Following the disappointing council, Koorland sought to find a little time for reflection before returning to the command bridge and the demands of his rank. Ever since he had taken up the mantle of Lord Commander it had seemed that vexation had become his constant companion.

He walked the corridors and decks of the *Alcazar Remembered*, but despite recent familiarity with the battle-barge it felt alien and unwelcoming. It was a ship of the Fists Exemplar, the demesne of Thane. As welcome as Koorland had been made, as much as he shared gene-seed with Thane and his battle-brothers, it was still foreign to an Imperial Fist.

His unthinking route took him away from the main decks and up towards the Navigation suite where the members of the Navis Nobilite were quartered. He did not disturb the Navigators, but turned towards the observation deck aft of their chambers. From the long starboard gallery of armourglass windows he could see Ullanor past jutting gun batteries below, the edge of a purple-grey hemisphere.

He looked at the planet for some time, no single thought coalescing, his mind moving from one concern to the next without even seeking solution – simply cataloguing the obstacles that seemed to have amassed in his path.

The thud of a heavy tread caused him to turn, expecting to see a maintenance servitor or other menial. Instead he met the concerned gaze of Maximus Thane.

'I apologise for the disturbance, Lord Commander,' said the Chapter Master. 'The fleet commanders and our battle-brothers have been requesting instruction. Did you learn anything more of use from the lord primarch?'

Koorland shook his head.

'We have not spoken further. It is clear he wishes me to fulfil the role of Lord Commander. The title is not for decoration alone even with his return.'

'I have issued standard protocols, in your name,' Thane

said, stopping alongside the Lord Commander. 'Straightforward requests for data, obvious fleet manoeuvres to allow the Adeptus Mechanicus to conduct survey flights. Bohemond and his Black Templars are assuming an aggressive orbital stance. It seems he is volunteering to be the spearhead of an assault.'

'Of course he is,' murmured Koorland. He waved a hand towards Ullanor and raised his voice. 'Against what foe should we cast the spear, Maximus? Would Bohemond have us strike without sight? If only I had the eyes to pierce the gloom that shrouds this world.' He turned away from the view and addressed Thane directly. 'What matter do you need to raise?'

'Something I think you need to know, though I cannot say if it is important or not. Events at Vandis that have been overlooked. The last transmission of Magneric – it has been gnawing at me. He was willing to risk everything to ensure it was safely conducted to Terra, but the ships had not arrived before our departure. Information so vital an honoured veteran of the Heresy War was prepared to make common cause with accursed traitors!'

'There is nothing I can do about that, brother.' Koorland sighed. 'I cannot reach out my hand and pluck the missing ships from the warp, nor pull free from them the information in an encrypted data-packet.'

'It is... an unfinished business,' Thane said slowly, choosing his words carefully, finding it difficult to explain his thoughts. 'And Zerberyn did not return, even though we know that the *Dantalion* survived the battle. It is most uncharacteristic that he did not come to Terra immediately.

Our astropaths and Librarians sought for any sign of their approach before we departed but saw nothing.'

'It is possible that both Zerberyn and others arrived after...' The Lord Commander straightened, struck by a thought. He glanced at the planet below and then back to Thane. 'Perhaps we do have eyes to pierce this veil, Maximus.'

For the first time in many, many days, Koorland smiled.

Maximus Thane had never previously ventured into this part of the *Alcazar Remembered*. There had been no reason to intrude upon the private chambers set aside for the Librarius of the Fists Exemplar. It was with a brief moment of trepidation that he paused at the threshold to the deck, one hand on the bulkhead, the other on the pistol grip at his hip as though expecting attack.

'Is there something wrong, brother?' Chapter Master Odaenathus asked from behind.

Thane did not look back, but knew the eyes of his companions were on him – Koorland, Adnachiel, Asger Warfist, Quesadra and Issachar. In other circumstances it would be unthinkable for such a group of officers to be absent from their commands while in orbit over an enemy world, but the orks had shown no more intent to attack than when the fleet had first broken warp. The Imperial Navy were more than capable of fending off the disjointed assaults by individual ork battleships and opportunistic flotillas.

Saying nothing, Thane stepped through into the Librarius deck, expecting to sense some change in the atmosphere or mood. Aside from his own tension, there was nothing. He looked at the wards cast into the fabric of the walls and bulkheads, psychic-shielding runes wrought as much to keep out unwanted attention as they were to contain the power of the Librarians gathered within. Should the Geller fields fail in warp transit – itself a numbing proposition – the inner wards provided a sanctum within the ship from which psychic resistance might be staged.

At the heart of the deck was an amphitheatre, the Hall of Solace. The dome above it was formed of petal-like segments lined with crystalline channels and veins, the seemingly haphazard array of blue and grey lines having a mesmerising quality when Thane looked up at them. The Hall of Solace was usually a place of solitude and calm, but today it served a different purpose.

Nearly a score of Space Marine psykers, in many colours and of varying rank, had gathered aboard the *Alcazar Remembered* in the ten hours since the war council. Some he had met before, such as Rune Priest Thorild from Asger Warfist's Great Company and Lexicanium Gandorin of the Dark Angels, as well as several from the Imperial Fists successors that had gathered at Phall. Others, the gaunt-faced Blood Angel Redolphio and Carrigan Nos of the Crimson Fists among them, were known to him only by name.

Thane glanced at Koorland and received a nod of assurance from the Lord Commander. Neither had remarked on the absence of Vulkan – the primarch was keeping his own counsel for the time being and that suited Thane. As much as the presence of the lord of the Salamanders gave him heart, Thane was also slightly disturbed by Vulkan's occasionally fatalistic utterances.

'Shall we begin?' asked Vaniel, the Chief Librarian of the

Ultramarines, who had been tasked with orchestrating the psykers.

'Why are we here?' said Quesadra. With the others he sat on a curved bench close to one of the walls, looking down into the bowl of the Hall of Solace.

'As witnesses,' Vaniel replied. 'My brother Librarians and I shall be in communion with each other and I shall be the conduit. To break through the fog of ork psychic power that envelops Ullanor we shall all need to enter a trance-like state. It is possible we will not remember that which we encounter.'

'Though we will not touch on your minds directly,' added Redolphio, 'you are all warriors with strong will. Your mere presence in this place will act as a shield against disturbances and intrusions, allowing us to focus our efforts on silencing the ork psychic roar.'

'Very well, what do you require of us?' said Koorland.

'Nothing more than your attention and your patience, Lord Commander,' said Vaniel. He turned back to his companions, standing within the lines of a hexagrammic star laid into the deck with lines of lead, the cardinal points and intersections marked by jutting pillars of metal like candlesticks. Vaniel stood at the centre. Pauldrons scraped against each other as the rest of the Librarians came together in a circle around him, the space intended for half their number.

The Librarians bowed their heads. An aura of light filled the air around them, glowing from the nest of cables that splayed from the neck openings of their armour and pierced each of their heads – psychic hoods that amplified their powers. Thane realised he was holding his breath. He let it out slowly, not wishing to betray his sensitivity. His exhalation came as a faint mist. The hall had dropped several degrees in temperature. A thin rime of frost glittered at the hexagrammic nodes on the floor.

The other officers were intent on the unfolding scene below and did not spare him a glance.

Silence descended, the only sounds those of the ship around them, which quickly faded from thought. The gleam and glitter of psychic energy were made more sinister by the lack of accompanying noise. No word was spoken by the Librarians but Thane had a sense of conversation, of the connection between them growing, unseen and unheard. He listened to the whisper of their breaths, realising that they were coming together, every inhalation and exhalation moving into time with the others.

Thane leaned forward, intent. His eyes swept from one Librarian to the next, seeking any sign of strain. If anything, the psykers looked at peace, eyes closed, faces relaxed. He could see Vaniel only in profile, but the Chief Librarian's face was slightly uplifted, as though a heavenly body above drew his unseen gaze. His eyes moved back and forth under the lids, as if reading.

'Anger.'

The word was muttered, barely audible as it left Vaniel's lips, but it made Thane twitch in surprise.

'Immortal anger. Rage. A tempest.' Vaniel's mouth barely moved but the words grew in volume, amplified by the chamber, settling in Thane's thoughts more loudly than the Librarian's voice alone. A darkness passed over Vaniel's face, like the shadow of a cloud.

Thane blinked. He looked up, and the channels of psychic crystal in the dome glowed with a consistent pale blue light. The lumen strips in the walls were equally constant.

'A storm, a storm of wrath, a storm of fury.'

Thane felt it. Felt the anger that lapped at the minds of the Librarians like a tide breaking against a sea wall. The others sensed it too. They shifted in unease, their movement in the corner of his eye, but his attention fixated upon the psykers. He saw the shadow again, darker, lingering longer on the face of Vaniel. Thane wanted to speak out but knew that any disturbance not only threatened failure in the ritual but might compromise the psykers' defences.

A scrape just beside him drew his glance for just a moment. Gauntleted fingers drew back along the bench, leaving ragged marks. Thane realised it was his own hand. His jaw was clamped tight, aching.

It was not just Thane and his distaste for psykers. A noticeable tension permeated the chamber, emanating from the circle of Librarians. The Space Marine officers observing the ritual all felt what Vaniel felt, sensing the savagery of the orks as well as hearing his thoughts in their minds. A brutal urgency was pushing into Thane, quickening his hearts.

'Straining, raging, thrashing,' Vaniel rasped. His voice was becoming more guttural, his demeanour darkened. He bared his teeth, heavy gasps punctuating his snarled words. 'The great green powers us. The great green becomes us. We are the great green.'

The grunts and groans were not limited to the Ultramarines Chief Librarian. The other psykers channelled the primal spirit of the orks, their faces masks of bestial hate, hands forming claws or fists. Redolphio was banging the heels of his hands against his chest, each impact sending a jolt of energy through the others. Thane noticed that the Blood Angel's incisors seemed long, fang-like. He tore his eyes away for just long enough to steal a glance towards Valefor. The Blood Angels captain was alert, leaning forward on the bench.

A growl, long and low, reverberated around the dome. Though he could not say how he knew, Thane felt it emitted from the Rune Priest, Thorild. The Fenrisian's eyes were wide open, glowing red like embers. His beard and hair moved as though in their own breeze. The pulses of energy playing around the assembled Librarians' psychic hoods was tainted by green sparks.

'The city,' croaked Vaniel. His gaze moved slowly around the room, his body turning with it. 'The citadel. Gorkogrod. Temple of the Great... Green. A throne of rage. A blade awaits. Cannons... lie slumbering.'

As one, all of the Librarians jerked, straightening suddenly with throaty roars. Thane started in shock, and the clatter and whine of war-plate betrayed the reactions of the others.

'The Beast arises!' Vaniel hunched, arms hanging like an ape's limbs, lips drawn back to reveal teeth and gums darkened by psychic power. He threw back his head and lifted his hands high, a wordless howl bursting forth. 'Waaaaagh!'

Several of the others raised their voices in unison, creating a primordial shout that shook the hall physically and psychically.

Thorild stepped back, breaking the circle. His entire body was taut, thrumming with tension like the air around him.

Ceramite shattered as talons of scarlet lanced from the Rune Priest's fingertips.

Koorland drew his pistol and fired, the bolt hitting the Space Wolf in the back of the left arm, splintering war-plate.

'No!' bellowed Asger, smashing a shoulder into the Lord Commander, sending Koorland's next shot into the far wall.

Thorild leapt, and in that moment Thane saw what the Rune Priest had sensed a moment earlier.

Vaniel drew his combat blade and pistol in a fluid movement. Roaring incoherently, he attacked, firing bolts into the face of Carrigan Nos of the Crimson Fists while he drove the point of the knife into the throat of Redolphio. Two other Librarians fell onto their companions, battering with fists wreathed in green lightning, shrieking like foul greenskins.

The other Ultramarine in the circle, Adarian, threw out a hand. A golden gladius appeared in his fist, piercing the chest of one of the ork-maddened psykers. Thorild's claws sheared through the throat of Vaniel, almost severing his head. A detonation of jade energy erupted from the slain Chief Librarian. The shockwave hurled everyone to the ground with a howling wind and the clatter of armour. It slammed into the walls and dome where runes burned with a blinding green light for several seconds.

Thane felt himself at the centre of a storm, his body crushed by a tremendous weight, his thoughts tossed adrift by the psychic tempest. The primal roar flowed into him. Through him. He gritted his teeth, resisting the instinct to add his voice to the tumultuous bellow.

For an instant he was but one of countless billions, a single warrior in an immense army that bestrode the stars.

His voice was countless voices. Countless voices were his. A single shout, a unifying war cry that drove them all, that fuelled and was fuelled from the great green sea that swept away all in its path.

The pounding of his hearts filled his ears. A growl shook Thane, welling up from his throat.

He needed his weapons. He needed to fight, to dominate, to destroy.

'I am Maximus Thane,' he snarled, the words coming as though dragged from his lips. 'Chapter Master of the Fists Exemplar. Son of Dorn!'

This last declaration broke him free from the lure of the savage ork spirit unleashed by the Librarians. He recovered his wits to find himself lying face down on the hard floor. He remained there for several heartbeats, steadying his thoughts before he risked standing.

Slowly he pushed himself up.

Koorland was already on his feet. He advanced on the dazed psykers, a glance at Asger warning the Wolf Lord to stay back. Thorild pushed himself away from the bloody wreckage that remained of Vaniel, covered in gore. His claws had disappeared and he held up his hands as Koorland approached with purpose.

'Wait!' called Thane. 'I saw what happened.'

Koorland stopped. His eyes remained on Thorild.

'So did I, brother.' He motioned for Thorild to put down his hands. 'I think we owe you a blood debt, Brother Rune Priest. Our loss would have been greater today if not for your strength.'

'The great green... The ork psychic field is phenomenal,'

Thorild whispered. 'All-consuming. I wanted to embrace it, become it. To unleash the beast inside.'

'It was not simply the gestalt ork presence,' said Adarian. The Ultramarine gazed sorrowfully at what remained of his superior. 'It was focused, as through a lens. Not consciously directed, but... amplified?'

'It reminded me of something,' said Gandorin. He glanced at the surviving psykers, haunted, and received nods of agreement. 'But I am not sure what.'

'I do not know,' said Adarian, 'but I concur. The Great Beast, we felt it, just for an instant. An incarnation. A conquering spirit given giant form. All that it is to be an ork, made flesh. Nearly overwhelming.'

'But you resisted,' said Thane, regaining his feet. He looked at the others that had countered the ork insurgence. 'You fought back.'

'It met something more savage,' Thorild growled. He tapped his chest. 'Something in here it wasn't expecting, a little gift of my Fenrisian heritage.'

'I followed your call,' said Gandorin. A brief smile. 'Your howl was louder.'

'What of the city?' The question came from Odaenathus. The others had descended to the floor of the hall and waited just behind Thane and Koorland.

'Gorkogrod,' said Adarian. 'We all saw it. A towering edifice, dedicated to the essence of orkdom. The Great Beast is there, I am certain.'

'Where?' asked Koorland. 'Where is this "Gorkogrod"?'

'I cannot say,' said Adarian. The other psykers shook their heads and frowned.

'Which part of the sun blinds you when you look upon it?' explained Gandorin. 'The assault was both like a lens, and diffused. We have learnt nothing in return for the losses we have suffered.'

This sombre news was greeted with silence. Thane looked at the Librarians who had been slain. Good warriors, taken from the service of the Emperor in the worst circumstance – by the hands of their battle-brothers.

'We must shut down all psychic activity across the fleet,' said Koorland. 'If this was a deliberate counter-attack, the orks may target our Navigators or the primaris psykers of the Astra Militarum.'

'There are means and places for such precautions,' said Thorild. 'Librarius sanctums. Navigator safe-chambers. Of course, some might not be willing to go into isolation.'

'We will not offer them the choice,' Koorland said quietly.

'And the astropaths,' added Odaenathus. 'This close to Ullanor, we cannot risk any psychic pollution, even if the orks do not intend it.' He looked at the corpse of Vaniel and shook his head. 'If the will of an Adeptus Astartes Chief Librarian is not strong enough to resist, perhaps even being soul-bound to the Emperor is no defence against the rage of the Great Beast.'

Thane had not thought it possible for the mood in the hall to get any grimmer, but he discovered he had been wrong.

The *Cortix Verdana* hung like an inverted pyramid in orbit over Ullanor. The Adeptus Mechanicus war-forge bristled with weapon turrets and gun decks, but it was the activity in its eight flight bays that was the focus of attention. The

strategium was abuzz with clattering, chattering servitors, the air thick with sacred incense issuing forth from the environmental systems in preparation for the massed launch, touching the air with the mixed scent of oil and perfume.

Gerg Zhokuv had been installed into his primary motor array, a sprawl of jointed limbs and coiled wires that gave him the freedom to move about the vast strategium deck via overhead magnetic runners. The hum of his perambulations heralded his arrival at any particular station, prompting the tech-priest overseers to sharply deliver their reports without need for request.

Bursts of machine-intelligible vox-code mixed with lingua-technis, the high notes against a background symphony of droning and whirring cogitators, metriculators and logistographs. The bubble of phageolinear pipes keeping the servitors alive was nearly lost in the hiss of hydraulics from augmented magi and the crackle of static-filled vid-screens awaiting active livefeeds from the drop-craft about to descend into Ullanor's murky atmosphere.

'Where is the magos veridi-exactor? I demanded his presence seven hectosecs ago!' Zhokuv's voice snapped mechanically from two hundred speaker grilles across the strategium, momentarily blotting out all noise.

'He is en route, revered Spear of the Omnissiah,' Magos Delthrak replied from a few paces behind the dominus. Zhokuv's chief strategos was a bear of a man. His red robes barely contained the mountain of flesh and bionics within. Muscular bulges and angular jutting edges distorted the heavy fabric. The tread of metal-shod feet set the deck plates trembling with every step. Two finger-thin tentacular mechadendrites whirred out from niches between his shoulders. They gesticulated in agitation. 'He has reached the logical limit for useful competence, dominus. I am unsure what role you foresee him adequately fulfilling. Why even have him brought forth from the datacores of Pavonis Mons?'

'This is why I am the dominus and you are the strategos,' rasped Zhokuv, his voice emitting from the personal address system mounted into the cradle holding his pteknopic jar.

'I am the Barbarian's Advocate, mighty Sun of Vengeance. It is my duty to test your theories. You should not take my disagreements personally.'

'I do not. Your role I accept. We should ever guard against self-replication and self-verification. Your unbridled enthusiasm for your duties, on the other hand...'

A piercing siren and flashing amber lights announced the opening of the grand doors of the strategium. Each door weighed several tonnes, constructed of layered plasteel and adamantium, able to withstand atomic attack and the heaviest melta blasts. Immense engines built within the doors themselves growled into action, sliding open the massive portal. It was rare for them to operate. On this level alone there were six other smaller entryways into the strategium for the regular coming-and-going of tech-priests and menials, not to mention elevators, conveyors and two staircases linking the master deck to the other parts of the immense command core.

Against the white lumen glow beyond the doors a small figure appeared. It stood lopsided on three spindly legs, a barrel-shaped body and upper limbs currently hidden in the voluminous folds of a tech-priest's robe. A head, or what was left of one, topped the bizarre torso. As the outlandish figure moved into the strategium, light glinted from a single natural eye set into what had once been the man's forehead, surrounded by metal reinforcements, data-gathering spines and sensor globes.

The tech-priest stopped. His head rotated left and right several times and then his focus latched on to the dominus. He surged closer in a series of unbalanced bursts, skidding to a halt every few strides before propelling himself forward. Stopping a few metres from the overlord of the Cult Mechanicus forces, the tech-priest unfolded two crane-like arms and dipped bodily in an approximation of a bow.

'Magos dominus, profound apologies for the tardiness of my response.' The tech-priest's voice was artificially modulated, the bass intonation strained through mechanical processors. 'My navigational banks were uploaded with inaccurate charts of the *Cortix Verdana*. I had to inquire as to the correct route to the strategium several times. I hope I have not missed anything.'

'Launch will commence in two hectoseconds, Magos Laurentis,' Zhokuv replied. Quivering metal appendages waved the unstable tech-priest aside and the dominus zipped to the main command station at the centre of the master deck. He settled his carry cradle into a socket where a more able-bodied leader might have placed a command throne. He had no physical need to see the screens and displays; he could monitor all of the feeds directly through digital translation. However, the symbolism of being at the literal centre of all of the martial activity was not lost on Zhokuv.

If he had possessed a more traditional corporeal incarnation, this was where he would have sat.

A gaggle of servitors blurted out the latest status updates while more of their kind ambled forward and plugged the dominus' thicket of external interface attachments into the sockets piercing the command station. Laurentis and Delthrak arrived just as he settled his systems into the embracing mecha-consciousness of the *Cortix Verdana*'s primary systems. Above him an atmospheric outlet puffed a mist of pungent sacred incense into the air, responding to his subconscious desire to exhale at length.

'Phaeton Laurentis, one of only two witnesses to survive the denouement of the Ardamantua attack,' the dominus said to Delthrak, turning a sapphire lens towards the tech-priest, in answer to his strategos' earlier complaint. 'Aside from the personal experience, Magos Laurentis is also a repository for all of the data related to encounters with the *Veridi giganticus* since the Ardamantua attack. I understand that your lack of induction through the Magi Militarum might impair your ability to understand some of my thinking, but in this case I would think my reasoning requires no justification.'

'He is dysfunctional, of dubious sanity, dominus,' said Delthrak. He glared at Phaeton. 'Unreliable.'

'Thank you,' said Laurentis, taking no affront from his superiors' discussion in his presence. 'I have come to the conclusion that reliability is an overemphasised trait. The unreliable orks appear to be doing very well thus far, to the extent that the Omnissiah might learn much from them.'

'He also blasphemes,' Delthrak added. 'He was almost

disassembled, a blatant *neovagris* apostate. A corrupting influence.'

'The magos' unorthodoxy is one of his greatest strengths. He is irretrievably broken, but his insights into the waywardness of the *Veridi giganticus* behavioural model are essential integration material. Have you not assimilated his recent *Treatise on the Notional Benefits of Wrongness*?'

'One of my most radical tracts.' A grating sound which might have been a chuckle vibrated through Laurentis' speaker. 'Also my shortest. I shall perform a through-check study to see if there is a correlation between brevity and anti-hierarchal asceticism.'

'The launch commences in one hectosecond,' announced the dominus, cutting off any further response from his strategos. The alert passed through his system without effort, his meta-consciousness overridden by the automaton will of the *Cortix Verdana*. As Zhokuv uttered the words, binharic cant-code throbbed from interconsciousness and out through the massive starship, setting off alerts and status demands in a cascade effect. Two hundred and forty-eight servitors roused from dormancy at his call, secondary monitor systems on-lining as his crypto-engrams flowed into their machine bodies. It felt as though he multiplied, becoming a thousandfold incarnation of himself. 'All stations on final alert for launch!'

Delthrak and Laurentis were arguing about something, but Zhokuv ignored them, letting their words fall into a temporary memory bank for later review while he focused his will on the final preparations for the scanning mission.

Blocky triangles of gunmetal and black, the data-gatherers

sat on their launch catapults and awaited the last integration protocols for their human pilots. Mostly human. While
cortical automata and servitors were useful for many tasks,
it was near-impossible to replicate human ingenuity and
intuition in an artificial spirit. Given the circumstances – a
descent into the virtually unknown, looking for an as-yet-
unidentified location – logic alone would not be able to
highlight the location of the Great Beast.

While the pilots plugged in their data cables and connected their brains to the machine-spirits of their unarmed
craft, Zhokuv ran a thorough diagnostic of the surveyor
assimilation systems. Twelve independent data-streams
coalesced within the analytic framework and the dominus
did not want to leave any possibility of information corruption or mis-flow. The response from the orks was, given past
experience, likely to be rapid and lethal. The pilots had been
briefed as such, the dominus making an effort to explain
to them the value of their potential sacrifice, ensuring they
were cognisant both of the honour they received in being
assigned to such an important mission and the glory of the
Omnissiah that went with them.

'Two decaseconds to mission commencement. Final alert,
all stations. Propulsion, bring to full orbital stasis for launch.'

Energy grids rippled across the *Cortix Verdana*. To
Zhokuv it felt like a sudden rush of blood – as well as he
could remember having such a thing, it having been over
a century since anything resembling flesh had encased his
consciousness. Arrestor engines and stabiliser jets fired,
ensuring the massive starship was in absolute synchronous
orbit with the rotation of the world below. Even a few metres

out of place could render the octangulated data-feed useless, putting off readings by several kilometres or more.

Zhokuv allowed himself a moment of introspection. Fifty milliseconds, to be precise. The behemoth weight of the starship was nothing, just a fraction of its mass at the outer edges of Ullanor's gravity well, riding the line between spiralling into the depths and slinging out into deeper orbit.

He wondered if birds felt a similar sensation, poised gliding on a volcanic thermal, riding the invisible line between flying and crashing into the fires below. Plasma pulsed through the dominus' artificial hearts and electricity flared along wires like blood vessels. Eyes that could scan every range of radiation glared down at Ullanor, vexed by the miasma of atmospheric and artificial fugue.

'Clear for launch. Bay doors to vacuum lock. Final status transmissions readied.'

He noticed that his subordinates had fallen silent. All eyes in the strategium capable of moving from their workstations were turned upon the banks of the main displays, now crackling with dark shadows from the interior of the flight decks.

'Mission commence. Vent bays.' Zhokuv felt a slight thrill himself. He had wondered if, divorced of normal human hormones, he was still capable of excitement. Apparently he was, though the experience was purely intellectual anticipation rather than instinctive reaction.

Air rushed out into the waiting vacuum as the flight deck doors swiftly opened. On some of the screens a mixture of distant stars and the purple-grey cloud of Ullanor's sphere appeared from the visual feeds. A spike of light and radiation from full-spectrum monitors flared across others.

He silently recalled his final, personal instructions from Fabricator General Kubik.

'Ullanor is their heartworld, the key to unlocking the secrets of the ork gravitic teleporters. Secure that knowledge for the Cult Mechanicus and you shall be immortalised as a Techtrarch of Mars, saviour of our creed. Whatever happens, we must ensure the survival and future of Mars.'

'Blessings of the Omnissiah upon your datacores!' Zhokuv announced, letting forth the launch transmission codes. 'Unto the void, unto the unknown, the hopes of sacred Mars upon your shoulders!'

The launch catapults flared, hurling the recon craft into the darkness. Zhokuv felt their expulsion as a ripple across nonexistent skin, perhaps like a scorpupine ejecting its poisonous spines at a predator.

The blunt-nosed ships curved out and down from the *Cortix Verdana*, the momentum of their ejection taking them away while the gravity of the world pulled them down into meticulously-calculated entry patterns.

All was silent across Zhokuv's systems for nearly a whole second. The engines of the datacraft flared, and they surged towards the planet in a dispersing cluster of sparks against the grey of Ullanor.

CHAPTER FOUR

Ullanor – low orbit

The lighting in the chamber had been switched off, leaving it illuminated only by tall candles arranged in a circle. Banners hung in the shadows and before each was set a small altar on which company relics had been carefully laid – wargear from past heroes, trophies from slain foes, artefacts connected to the Emperor, Dorn and Sigismund.

'Upon us has been thrust a duty no other is willing to take.' Bohemond stood in the circle of light, in front of his kneeling marshals. His blade was bared, its edge resting on the skin of his exposed left palm. The light of the candles was swallowed by the black weave of his robe, his skin dark. 'We few, we that hold to the higher ideals of the Emperor from the wisdom of Sigismund, know a Truth far more valuable than any weapon.'

His seven subordinates looked up at him with expressions fierce with pride, eyes alight with zealous fury.

'Long has been the path to this understanding, long have we warred in the darkness driven by ancient oath but unknowing of the Truth to which we were being drawn. As the Light of the Emperor guides ships in the warp, we must allow the Truth to guide our actions. Only from the divine will of the Master of Mankind comes our purpose. No loyalty, no oath, no duty is above that fealty.'

He slowly drew the blade across his hand, allowing thick blood to spill onto the parchment that lay on the deck at his feet, weighted with gilded skulls of assorted alien species – an ork among them. The blood spattered across the yellowing sheet and soaked into the porous material. Moving his hand, Bohemond allowed the drop to form a rough cross, the shape of the Black Templars Chapter badge.

'From this blood we shall know the Truth, for the Emperor's Will courses through our veins. Our hearts beat by His design. Lord Dorn, our creator's eternally blessed son, gave unto Sigismund his gene-seed and from Sigismund the Great and the Loyal Crusade we were given form and will.'

Bohemond flicked his blade clean, the last of the blood creating fresh marks on the parchment. He sheathed the sword and crouched, examining the patterns in some detail. The High Marshal allowed the Truth to take him, his stare losing focus, his vision fogging as the spirit of the Emperor seeped into his soul, touching him with its wisdom.

The markings swam in his vision, merging and splitting, forming shapes as yet beyond discerning. Bohemond closed his eyes, allowing the memory of the blood-omens to continue to form in his thoughts, seeking the intervention of his divine master.

It came to him in a flash. The patterns became an image, the image a vision. A sword descending, piercing a world.

Its meaning was clear.

'Praise the Emperor, for He has made His will known to us!' declared Bohemond, opening his eyes.

'Mark these words for remembrance, brothers!' he whispered, looking at each of his subordinates, pleased by their resolve. 'Trust in the Emperor at the hour of battle. Trust to Him to intercede, and protect His warriors true as they deal death on alien soil. Turn their seas to red with the blood of the slain. Crush their hopes, their dreams, and turn their songs into cries of lamentation.'

At a gesture from their High Marshal the Black Templars rose. Bohemond stooped and picked up the parchment. He tore it into strips, passing the tatters to his subordinates. Clermont fell out of line to follow his commander, bringing with him one of the large red candles that illuminated the chamber. Using the molten wax, he helped his battle-brothers to affix the bloodied parchment to their armoured pauldrons, placing each piece amongst the remains of previous purity seals.

'Praise the Emperor. In our blood flows His will,' each marshal intoned as he received the anointment from Clermont. 'As our blood flows, His will is done.'

'Return to your ships and prepare for the combat drop,' Bohemond announced. 'We have enough data from the initial scans to target the enemy. Let others wring their hands like timid scholars pondering their mysteries. We are the light that leads the way. The crusade continues, brothers! We are the Black Templars, the Emperor's Sword, and in our wake shall come the Imperial Truth.'

'We attack, High Marshal?' asked Clermont. The castellan

was excited by the prospect, not daunted. His hands trembled with anticipation, spilling drops of wax from the candle.

Bohemond smiled.

'Indeed! Let us pray, as our bolters shall praise the Emperor soon enough.' He bowed his head, one hand on the pommel of his sword, for no true warrior could commune with the Emperor without a weapon in hand. 'Lead us from death to victory, from falsehood to truth. Lead us from despair to hope, from faith to slaughter. Lead us to His strength and an eternity of war. Let His wrath fill our hearts. Death, war, and blood – in vengeance serve the Emperor and the name of Dorn!'

The initial readings had been fruitful but not conclusive. Skimming through the upper atmosphere, the datacraft pieced together a rudimentary topology and energy schematic of Ullanor. The world was made up of three large continents and two oceans, one broken by a vast archipelago. These bodies of water were shallow, scarcely seas at all, and what further water remained to the planet was mostly trapped at the icy poles. The land was covered with urban sprawl, almost four-fifths of Ullanor inhabited, the density rising to an estimated several hundred thousand per square kilometre in the areas defined by the orbital surveys. It was to these huge conurbations that the datacraft headed, dividing into squadrons as they descended several kilometres through the thick clouds of vapour and pollutants.

'Why have the orks not attacked?' asked Delthrak. 'We know that they possess detection systems capable of reaching beyond orbit.'

'Insufficient data,' chimed three of the dominus' servitors before he could reply.

'Our craft are unarmed. Perhaps they do not perceive them as a threat,' Zhokuv said.

'Orks care nothing for such niceties,' countered Laurentis. A cable snaked from the nape of his neck to a nearby console, allowing him to monitor the dataflow in real time. 'They relish conflict but they are also genetically programmed to dominate and destroy. However, there may be another truth hidden in your words, dominus. The lack of armament may mean the orks simply do not recognise the datacraft. It would be inconceivable to their minds that an aerocraft would not possess weapons. They might simply mistake them for orbital debris.'

As he considered this, Zhokuv slid a partial-consciousness engram through a data-transmitter, allowing him to settle part of his awareness into the implants of one of the pilots' brains. For this close inspection he chose the lead craft of the squadron nearing the largest energy returns. Only the complete rejection of the flesh allowed him such transference – bitter experience had taught some of his body-bound predecessors that biological distraction acted as an anchor to the consciousness and caused duality-matrix problems with full engrammic integration.

Zhokuv reminded himself that he had transitioned to total pteknopic encasement to allow him to better monitor the battle-data for his command, but the perk of being able to partially experience front-line conflict in this manner also brought a certain level of satisfaction and reward.

The pilot blinked as the dominus' presence settled into

his stem implants. Zhokuv adjusted his perception systems, dialling them back to the mortal visual spectrum, and looked out of the pilot's eyes. Witnessing an event first-hand was as important as any data-feed analysis.

The squadron broke through the cloud layer just a short time later, revealing the sprawl of the ork cities and the wastelands between. Grey dunes spread across steep hills and dells, shifting in a strong crosswind. Large patches of oxide red and verdigris-like debris marked the expanse. Processing this, Zhokuv determined that the colouration was due to staining from the decay of ancient metals – possibly structures, potentially immense machines.

This ashen wilderness was littered with fortresses and other defensive structures. Walled compounds several kilometres across loomed over fading lines of age-old highways, while spurs of stone parapet and turrets splayed like the limbs of squatting arachnids, tipped with ungainly towers of corroded metal.

Sluggish rivers of polluted water meandered through the detritus-citadels. Spectromatic feedback revealed a toxic combination of chemicals oozing from the city, acidic and deadly – at least, to humans. Though he understood the hardiness of the orkoid species, the dominus was surprised to see small towns clinging to the banks of the rivers, breaching the lakes and pools as stilt-villages, as though some sustenance might be clawed back from the oil-slicked flows.

The outer settlements and maze of roads grew thicker closer to the city, like the moons of a gas supergiant unable to escape its pull, not yet consumed by its presence. There was no single point of change, no easy delineation between not-city and city. The citadels started to merge, becoming vaster and taller, yet still only outskirts and buttresses of the urban mountain that rose up beyond.

While he rode on the physical senses of the datacraft pilot, the dominus allowed his central consciousness capacitors to analyse the ongoing stream of other data fed into dozens of the *Cortix Verdana*'s supracogitators. He traced a near-invisible energy stream, networking through the scattered settlements to the central mass of the city itself. There was certainly no sign of a physical transmission system on the surface, and the surveyors were unable to determine if subterranean lines carried the energy waves. Nor did there seem to be any specific generation point. A few reactors and power plants had been detected in some of the fortresses, but their grids did not extend far beyond their walls.

More confusingly, the energy flow appeared to be towards the city, not out of it. The settlements were *feeding* the city somehow.

With a growing sense of distasteful revelation, Zhokuv was forced to conclude that the city was built from the remains of a far larger settlement, like a star going nova that was consuming its stellar system to fuel itself. Its near-impossible bulk heaved out of the plain, separated from a high mountain range to the west by a broad river that meandered north-west to a ragged coastline fifteen kilometres from the base of the mountain.

Tecto-sonographic impulses revealed that the heart of the city delved as deep into the crust as it rose, a catacomb of thousands of square kilometres of halls and corridors, the equal of the buildings and streets above.

Unlike the shanty-keeps of the ash wastes, these buildings seemed new. Although the materials were obviously reclaimed, showing signs of corrosion and improvisation, the slab-sided structures had a more considered, fabricated look than the ad-hoc fortifications of the wasteland. The closer to the centre of the city, the more organised the layout. Wide thoroughfares and broad plazas that would be the envy of any Imperial city emerged from the discordant urban clutter of the periphery.

Even as he marvelled at this, Zhokuv registered a vocal input and identified it as coming from Phaeton Laurentis.

'Remarkable,' droned the tech-priest. 'Even a cursory analysis of the structural integrity ratings reveals a complex logarithmic progression.'

'I see it,' said Delthrak. 'It is an exponential inversion. What does that mean?'

'Order from anarchy.' Laurentis let out one of his grating chuckles. 'An urban incarnation of the emergence of will over wild.'

The dominus briefly focused on the other squadrons, to see if they encountered similar circumstances. The other two cities, of which it seemed there were actually many more across the planet, duplicated the structure-from-disorder scale to varying degrees.

'Manifest order!' crowed Laurentis. His enthusiasm quickly turned to solemnity. 'I warned about this from the outset. But I was wrong, no simple will guides this. No volition. No single vision, to be precise. It is the inherency of the native orkoid hierarchy to eventually escalate to a point where upper echelons of order realise endemically out of the semi-random appropriation of their genetic and tech-nological inheritance.'

'If allowed to grow to sufficient levels, a true *Veridi gigan-ticus* civilisation emerges?' Zhokuv mused. 'A sustainable, organised culture? Is that really possible?'

'Possibly even sentience to the point of co-existence,' Lau-rentis postulated, his vocal synthesisers tremulous with the thought.

'Impossible,' snapped Delthrak. The Barbarian's Advocate snorted. 'Highly organised, I grant you. Capable of peace-ful interaction with other species? Nothing in any study has ever hinted at such a possibility. Structured or not, they would see the Cult Mechanicus and humankind destroyed or enslaved.'

'No weapons,' added the dominus. 'We are well within any security zone, eighteen kilometres from the city cen-tre. No response as yet...'

Long-range visuals started to reveal the innermost areas of the city, while laser-like injection scans sent back more detailed feedback of geological, physical and structural data.

Where the outer precincts seemed heaped upon each other, almost toppling upon themselves in their efforts to cram in as much living space as possible, the city's inner region was like the eye of a storm.

An instant later Zhokuv's surveyor-senses felt a surge of power from below, emanating from the outer fortifications. His immediate reaction set sirens squealing through the decks of the *Cortix Verdana* and triggered alarms across the panels of the other datacraft. The pilot he was monitoring

responded within moments, as did the others, but human reactions were simply not swift enough to avoid what happened next.

Energy flared up from the ground, flowing like a shimmering wall from hundreds of generator stations located in the outlying citadels. Four milliseconds after first detecting the eruption, Zhokuv wrenched his engrammatic presence out of the pilot's body, but even so he felt the contact-shock of the force field's interaction with the datacraft.

Through his assayer conduits on the *Cortix Verdana* the dominus witnessed an interspersed energy signature unlike anything he had encountered – part gravitic, part electromagnetic, part radiation, and part something entirely unquantifiable. The same happened in the other targeted cities, with near-instantaneous coordination between the different conurbations.

Part of him experienced the raising of the defensive shield in this detached manner, watching the intersection of the roiling wave with the physical entities of the datacraft, slicing them in half. Simultaneously, his meta-being still encapsulated in the biological systems of the pilot caught the faintest echo of the man's interpretation of events.

It was as though a giant hand swatted him out of the sky. An impression, nothing physical to be recorded, nothing verifiable. *Swatted*. It was the exact feeling that vibrated through Zhokuv's being as the tiniest portion of mortal pain started to flood the pilot's nervous system and the dominus' engrammatic ejection completed.

The datacraft and its companions exploded as power plants overloaded, turning each into a scattering of particles that slicked along the shimmering screens of energy that now enveloped the cities.

Wholly back aboard his starship, Zhokuv took nearly two seconds to recover from the shock of engrammatic death. He felt incomplete, disjointed. Flustered, he withdrew his other data-tendrils from the *Cortix Verdana*'s systems, allowing full control back to the servitors and tech-priests. He detached his auditory and visual inputs to cocoon himself in absolute sense deprivation for several milliseconds while he contemplated the experience.

Mortality. There had been no physical threat to the dominus but even the glancing experience of the orks' power left him in no doubt that he faced a highly advanced technology. It was one matter to know as much from the reports of the attack moons and other weaponry thus far employed, but it was something far different to encounter it first-hand.

Shock gave way to remembrance of his duty to the Cult Mechanicus. Fear subsided, to be replaced with resolution and ambition.

The power arrayed against them was indeed formidable, but he would overcome the obstacles. Zhokuv would harness that power and tame the xenos technology, for the sake of Mars.

CHAPTER FIVE

They must find their own way, so thinks the father. Mistakes teach us, experience moulds us. Who am I to deny them this? I learnt at the feet of two fathers, and still my mistakes were grievous. I trusted. I hoped. I dreamed.

The dream became a nightmare.

Let them find their own path, wayward and wandering. They do not need my dreams to guide them astray.

Staring out of the canopy of the Thunderhawk's cockpit, Bohemond could see the blazing entry trails of the other gunships streaking down to the surface. For a time he watched the falling stars of destruction, bright lights against the perfect deep blue of near space.

'It is beautiful,' he whispered.

'The Emperor's vengeance on swift wings, High Marshal,' replied Eudes, in the piloting position next to Bohemond. The jet black of his armour was marked by a single red pauldron on the left, signifying his symbolic ties to Mars as a Techmarine.

'We are the guiding light and the burning flame, brother. On our blades the xenos will learn the penalty for despoiling the Emperor's realm. Bolt and plasma, sword and fist shall be the manner of their punishment.'

'Glorious fate, High Marshal, to be chosen amongst the Emperor's anointed warriors!' crowed Eudes. 'Those that come after shall envy us this opportunity to strike in righteousness and end the terror of the greenskins forever.'

'Indeed they shall. The Great Beast is no such thing. A petty alien warlord preying on fools that allowed self-service to outweigh diligence. The orks are a judgement upon the laxity of the High Lords. Before the blood of the invaders has soaked into the soil of the lands they have despoiled we shall bring the Emperor's scorn upon the vermin that infest Holy Terra.'

'Is that not the task of the Inquisition, High Marshal?' Eudes glanced at his commander.

Bohemond watched the flicker of plasma jets disappear into the thickening cloud bank. A few seconds later the cockpit dimmed, the view outside turned to a uniform purple-grey of diffused light. His gaze moved to the surveyor screens, the transponder positions of the other Thunderhawks marked out by red sigils on the black display. In arrowhead formation they continued to plunge surfaceward.

'The Inquisition?' Bohemond resisted the urge to spit his disgust. 'Cloistered meddlers, products of the inbred politics of the Senatorum.'

'Of course, High Marshal.' Eudes paused, uncertain of continuing.

'You think that I overstep the mark of an Adeptus Astartes commander, Eudes?'

'There are covenants, oaths...'

'Pledges are but one form of honour and duty, brother. Ours is a higher cause, our judge none other than the Emperor Himself. What mortal bondage can stay our hand when a higher calling demands action? If I had been chosen as Lord Commander our forces would not be loitering in orbit as uncertain as a novitiate at first bolter drill. Praise Vulkan, son of the Emperor, but he is not the Emperor Himself. His coddling of Koorland leads our crusade astray.'

Eudes said nothing, fixing his eyes upon the monitors and controls. He was clearly ill at ease with the words of his superior but he offered no argument that might be taken as insubordination.

'A doubt unvoiced is a doubt doubled,' said the High Marshal.

'Why must we hide the Truth, Brother-Marshal?' Eudes' look was plaintive. 'Why should we be ashamed of being the Emperor's trusted heralds?'

'Be wary, brother.' Bohemond spoke softly. He laid a hand upon the arm of his companion, a gesture of solidarity and reassurance. 'The Emperor has chosen us to bear this message, because we are strong enough. The others are weak. They hold His light but do not embrace it. We are the true fists of the Emperor, the inheritors of the crusade He launched across the stars. In time others will come to our cause and know the truth of it. The Master of Mankind hid His light for thousands of years until the time was right to lead humanity back to glory. What terrible labour

is it to conceal our greatness for a few years so that revelation might come at the correct moment?'

'You are right, High Marshal. It was selfish of me to doubt your wisdom.'

'The wisdom of Sigismund, not mine. We are great because we are the sons of greatness, never forget that.'

For the next several minutes Bohemond studied the navigational data transmitted by the Adeptus Mechanicus, gathered by their scout flights just before the datacraft had been destroyed. There was barely a square kilometre of the surface that was not populated – and hence defended. Wherever the Black Templars landed they would face instant retaliation. The only plausible attack strategy was to make planetstrike in overwhelming force, obliterating the orks in the landing zone's vicinity to allow Bohemond's warriors to establish a working beachhead.

He reviewed possible strike locations, immediately dismissing any landing within one of the major cities. As tempting as it was to directly pierce the heart of the enemy, there was little reward in attacking the most heavily fortified areas. Instead, his thoughts were drawn to one of many strange expanses in the ash wilds – areas obviously artificially flattened but bereft of significant structures. It was likely they were sites for future settlements, cleared and prepared but the construction not yet commenced.

A signal alerted him to a communication incoming from the *Abhorrence* in orbit. He activated the Thunderhawk's vox-systems. Through the hiss of distance and growing interference from Ullanor he recognised Clermont's voice.

The castellan had been left in command of the fleet assets, awaiting instruction on the primary landing site.

'High Marshal, we are losing surveyor contact with your position,' the castellan warned. 'I have been told communications will deteriorate rapidly over the next five minutes, possibly be eliminated entirely.'

'You need the target zone, yes?'

'Affirmative, High Marshal. Our companies are waiting in their drop pods, the cascades are primed for launch. Do we have an assault site confirmed?'

Bohemond looked again at the rough cartographic intelligence. One site looked the same as any other from their current position. He closed his eyes and adjusted the viewscreen without looking, trusting in the Emperor to lead him to the best site, a silent prayer for guidance in his thoughts. He opened his eyes and picked the closest of the flat expanses, noting the grid reference.

'Transmitting target data to you, brother-castellan.' Bohemond entered the coordinates and despatched an encrypted signal to the *Abhorrence*. 'Immediate drop. Your assault wave will make planetfall no more than three minutes after our touchdown.'

'We have your target data, High Marshal. Confirmed that assault wave will make planetfall at the target location in twenty-eight minutes.' The link crackled for several seconds and then Clermont spoke again. 'I have, per your orders, informed the Lord Commander of our intent to secure a landing zone and asked for his support. I have also contacted the other commanders. Quesadra, Antilipedes and Valefor have pledged support for the attack, and I will pass on the target data as soon as we launch. Issachar has made a qualified promise of secondary attack, dependent upon his review of the landing zone data. Odaenathus will only act on orders from the Lord Commander. I assume the Salamanders will follow Vulkan's will, whatever that turns out to be. I have yet to receive responses from the others.'

'Have you heard from Thane or Koorland?'

'The Lord Commander has contacted us. I passed him the same information as the others, but he demands to speak with you. I have a vox-feed ready to link if you are willing, High Marshal.'

'Very well, brother, I will speak with him. Continue with the assault as planned.'

The vox snarled and hissed for a few more seconds and then went quiet, signifying contact had been established with the *Alcazar Remembered*.

'Lord Commander, you are speaking to High Marshal Bohemond.'

'I demand that you call off your planetstrike immediately, Bohemond!' Koorland sounded strained, though the poor quality of the link might also have been responsible for the flutter in his voice. 'You have no authority to launch this attack.'

'I am High Marshal Bohemond of the Black Templars, recognised as Chapter Master by the Senatorum Imperialis. I know well how far my authority extends, and yours, Lord Commander.'

'We cannot attack piecemeal, brother.' Koorland's attempts at conciliation sounded equally as forced as his assumed authority. 'We must coordinate our strategy with the Astra Militarum and Adeptus Mechanicus. This impetuous assault will gain us nothing.'

'You wish to talk of strategy, Lord Commander? You said yourself that we can do nothing from orbit. Why waste time? The longer we hold back our fury the more we allow the orks opportunity to prepare their defences. We are the Space Marines of the Emperor. We lead, others follow. Koorland, it is time to lead!'

Koorland did not reply immediately, the delay in transmission caused by more than simple distance. It was in such moments that Bohemond was pleased to possess the Light of the Emperor. Hesitation was doubt made manifest and he harboured no doubts. Listening to the static, Bohemond thought the Lord Commander might hear the thoughts of the Master of Mankind, hoped that perhaps the divine will made itself manifest in the mind of the Imperial Fist.

Evidently, it did.

'We will launch a full assault in support of your attack.' Koorland's sigh was just about audible. The vox-link was worsening by the second.

'It is a wise commander tha–'

'By my word, Bohemond, this matter is not concluded. You are subject to my command and specific orders will be forthcoming.'

The vox-hiss was almost overwhelming.

'Affirmative, Lord Commander. For the Emperor!'

Any reply Koorland might have made was lost in the surge of static. Bohemond turned to Eudes and smiled.

'Justice prevails. The Emperor provides, brother.' He switched the vox to general address, his words carrying to the hundred Black Templars of the strike force. 'We are dark vengeance clad in light. We are the purging of the weak. We are the irresistible ending. Glory to the sons of Sigismund, for the Emperor has seen fit to deliver us in righteousness to the heart of the cause.

'What happy tidings, that we be so blessed by the Emperor to stand upon the brink of His vengeful storm, the lightning that shall strike His foes asunder. He that outlives this day, and comes safe home, will stand taller when this day is named, and rouse him at the name of Ullanor. He that shall live this day, and see old age, will yearly on the vigil toast his companions, and say "Tomorrow is the Remembrance of Ullanor." Then will he strip his sleeve and show his scars, and say "These wounds I had on Ullanor." And all will rejoice in his glory. The Emperor watches us, brothers. No fear. No pity. No remorse!'

Kilometres above, the drop bays of a dozen Black Templars battle-barges and strike cruisers opened. They coughed forth the second assault wave and the battle for Ullanor began.

Koorland pounded his fist on the plasteel of the door, the blows echoing down the corridor, resounding within the chamber.

'Lord Vulkan!' He slammed his hand against the door again, already irritated by the primarch's lack of response to his vox-hails. 'Lord Vulkan!'

Gears wheezed and the door cranked open, revealing the primarch standing at the threshold with one hand on the controls, towering over the Lord Commander. Koorland stepped back, his agitation suddenly cowed by the dominating presence.

'There is a reason I have not answered your communications, Lord Commander Koorland,' growled the primarch. He turned away and Koorland relaxed slightly, as though released from an invisible grip. Vulkan waved towards his work bench where his hammer lay on the top, the innards of its head splayed across the surface. 'I have my own labours to attend to. What is so urgent that it demands my personal attention?'

'The attack on Ullanor has begun.'

'That seems... precipitous. I have monitored the data-channels, I saw no indication that the location of the Great Beast has been identified. Where are you attacking?'

'Bohemond has launched an assault on the planet.' Koorland uttered the words as calmly as possible, not wishing to show discomfort in front of the primarch. He swallowed hard, his annoyance at Bohemond's challenge to his authority overtaking his vexation at Vulkan's self-imposed solitude.

'A reconnaissance-in-force, Lord Vulkan,' he continued. 'Adeptus Astartes companies will secure ground and then we will establish the location of the Great Beast from intelligence gathered on the surface. The Adeptus Mechanicus and Astra Militarum will commit their forces when the primary target is located.'

Vulkan raised his eyebrows as he looked back, leaning over the table. His fingers continued to work at the exposed cables of his weapon, pushing them back into the head of Doomtremor.

'You are making a landing without exact knowledge of the Great Beast's whereabouts?'

'I...' Koorland had nothing to offer. He shook his head and looked away, unable to meet the primarch's inquiring look. 'The initiative was Bohemond's, not mine, lord primarch.'

'I see.' Vulkan finished his work quickly and set his hammer aside. He pulled forward a screen on an articulated arm and his fingers danced over the runepad below. Without looking at him, Vulkan gestured for Koorland to approach. 'These are the findings from the Adeptus Mechanicus flights, yes?'

Koorland looked at the screen and nodded.

'There are still three possible sites,' he said. 'Nothing pinpoints a specific location. All we have from the psychic scan is a name. Gorkogrod. The landing is blind, to all intents. Interference is still wreaking havoc with surveyors and communications. The only option is to seek out what we want on the ground. We can take prisoners, find out where Gorkogrod is located.'

'A justification, after the event,' Vulkan said quietly. 'Bohemond has forced you into premature action. He has already chosen your "only option".'

'Perhaps,' conceded Koorland. He clenched a fist. 'We cannot afford the luxury of blame at this moment. What has happened cannot be changed. The consequences have to be dealt with. Bohemond has a point, lord primarch. Time is not our ally. We must commit to action sooner rather than later. We do not know how long until the orks attack Terra again. Perhaps even now the Throneworld is assaulted.'

Vulkan held his hand up to the flickering screen, as if

communing with it, fingers not quite touching its surface. His brow knotted in thought and relaxed.

'Here,' he declared. 'This is Gorkogrod. Here you will find the Great Beast.'

Koorland looked. Vulkan had chosen one of the cities approached by the Adeptus Mechanicus flights. By coincidence, it was the closest to Bohemond's impending planetfall.

'Are you sure, Lord Vulkan? Why this one?'

Vulkan looked sharply at him and he flinched, fearing he had angered the primarch.

'Is my word not enough, Lord Commander Koorland?'

'Should it be?' Koorland asked cautiously. He had no desire to anger the primarch further, quite the opposite, but Vulkan's manner and actions since his return had been erratic. 'I do not mean to doubt your word, Lord Vulkan. There is so much at stake, I need to be certain. How can you know that this is the place?'

'You must learn to show a little faith, Koorland.' Vulkan pushed away the screen and folded his arms. 'And you must also learn that certain things happen in a certain way. War has a pattern, a form. It follows specific paths to known ends. We seek confrontation with the Great Beast. That confrontation will occur. The narrative of war demands it.'

'I still don't understand. What narrative? War is not a story, Lord Vulkan.'

'War is always a story, Koorland, told by the victors, shaped by the survivors.' The primarch sighed, not in frustration but resignation. 'The orks respect only power. To defeat the orks requires a greater power. Our presence here, our attack, is a challenge to the Great Beast. Never forget that it is an ork, nothing more. It must prove itself, it can do nothing but show its dominance over a foe. It can no more resist the lure of battle than a predator can resist the urge to pounce for the kill.'

'That does not explain how you can know that this city is Gorkogrod, Lord Vulkan.'

'More than fifteen hundred years ago, the Great Crusade of the Emperor came to this world. Horus himself bested the warlord that ruled here, and a great triumph was held in honour of the victory. On this world, the orks were broken. On this world, humans proved their dominance.'

'And the orks have reclaimed it...' Koorland moved past the primarch and looked at the conglomeration of lines and figures that denoted the ork city. 'This world was lost again generations ago, but nobody noticed. The orks have taken it back. But there is something more. Zhokuv's tech-priests posit that this latest expansion is a new phase of war. The cities have cannibalised smaller settlements to grow.'

'A catalyst, a signal,' said Vulkan. 'Symbols matter, Koorland, especially to the primitive minds of the orks. The narrative, the story of Ullanor. One rises, others follow, greater than any for fifteen hundred years. Where would such a creature build its capital?'

Koorland considered the question, trying to imagine the thought processes of an ork. To prove it was the most powerful, it had to overcome the biggest foe, be the most important thing on the planet.

'The Triumph...' Koorland looked at the screen again. 'This is where the Triumph ended?'

Vulkan nodded.

'Here the Emperor stood, greatest warlord of all time. Here nine of His sons stood, lauding their father. Here He named Horus as Warmaster. We know what happened next.' Vulkan tapped the screen, the sound like a normal man's fist thudding against a window. 'Places remember such events. Worlds are marked by the passing of such beings. Where the Emperor treads, legends follow. Where else would an ork civilisation start? Where else but at the very place where it ended?'

'Yes, I see it,' said Koorland. He activated a vox-link to the command bridge. 'Thane, Gorkogrod has been located. Inform the fleet, we have a target point.'

The narrative of war. The story of the orks. He looked at Vulkan, marvelling at the primarch's perception. It seemed obvious in reflection, as most great insights did.

Where would the tale of Ullanor move next? What other chapters would unfold before a new legend had been created?

CHAPTER SIX

Ullanor – low orbit

The main flight deck of the cruiser *Divine Right* thrummed with idling engines and echoed to the clatter of ratchet cranks and the whine of loader servitors fitting hellstrike missiles to the wings of six Lightning air superiority fighters. Tech-priests performed their final chants and benedictions, activating the machine-spirits of the aircraft in turn. They formed into two lines flanking the path from the pilots' quarters – a guard of honour, censers spilling fragrant smoke, oil-tipped rods raised in salute to those that would guide the machines down to Ullanor.

Six silver-masked figures emerged from the ruddy gloom of the suiting chamber. Their dark-blue flight suits bulged with pressure lines and reinforcement studs. Two acolytes of the Cult Mechanicus fell in step behind each of the anointed air-warriors, murmuring the blessings of the Machine-God upon their life support systems, daubing the holy oils of Mars onto the rubberised skin of their suits.

Thus consecrated to guide the vessels of the Omnissiah,

the pilots climbed up the ladders of their machines while the engines of the Lightnings were fired by ignition rods. The idling of motors intensified to a growl. Final rites were grated by vocalisers and modulated tongues, praising the artifice of man and the beneficence of the Machine-God. Armoured canopies whined closed, sealed with elongated hisses.

The tech-priests and their semi-aware attendants rapidly left the flight deck, vacuum-proof heavy doors sealing the bay behind them. Red lights flashed in warning as the outer portal opened like a castle portcullis rising, the trapped air evacuating into the void in a gale.

Jets flaring, the Lightnings sped out one after the other, dipping towards the orb of Ullanor. From other ships across the fleet more scatters of plasma-jets were emerging, hundreds of craft speeding towards the planet.

A few dozen kilometres from atmospheric entry one of the Lightnings peeled away, guidance jets spitting fire as it veered towards the northern pole.

'Hiedricks? What are you doing?' demanded the squadron commander, Corbrus. 'Return to formation immediately!'

There was no response.

'I don't know how you conducted business aboard the *Impregnable*, Hiedricks, but in my squadron you obey immediately! Return to formation or we will shoot you down!'

The rogue Lightning's engines burned brighter as it accelerated. Corbrus' long-range vox crackled into life.

'Hawk squadron, report status,' came the inquiry from the *Divine Right*. 'We are monitoring an unauthorised manoeuvre.'

'The new pilot that came over from the *Impregnable*,

Hiedricks, just broke formation, command. Permission to pursue and engage.'

'Negative, mission takes precedence. Continue to allocated patrol coordinates and provide additional interception cover for Adeptus Astartes forces on the surface.'

'Understood,' replied Corbrus, reluctantly. He watched the last spark of the Lightning dipping towards atmospheric entry and consulted his nav-pad. At that trajectory, Hiedricks seemed to be heading directly for the major ork city, the one called Gorkogrod. If Hiedricks was deserting, he was picking the worst place possible to do it.

Twenty-two minutes later, Hawk Four swooped into the outskirts of Gorkogrod. A kilometre above the surface, the pilot ejected, leaving his aircraft to spear into the ork shanty surrounding the main city. Ammunition and hellstrike missiles detonated with a blast that levelled buildings for eighty metres, sending a pall of smoke and dust boiling into the thick air.

Deftly manipulated grav-chute suspensors carried the pilot away from the burning wreckage of his Lightning. He landed amongst a tangle of scrap and broken masonry where a cluster of buildings had recently been torn down. Several small greenskins that had been scavenging the debris snarled and spat at him as he landed, brandishing lengths of pipe and improvised daggers.

The pilot pulled free a needle pistol and opened fire, every shot putting a toxin-laden shard into the eye of each of the five gretchin. They spasmed as they fell, shrieks stifled by the blood bubbling from their lungs.

The man took off his helm and stripped off the flight suit, revealing muscle-cladding synskin. It rippled as he activated its cameleoline coating, the surface becoming a blur of metallic shades and dark brown. He gathered up the corpses of the dead aliens and thrust them beneath a sheet of corrugated steel.

Retrieving several other weapons he had concealed within the pilot's gear, Esad Wire hid the uniform with the bodies and set off towards central Gorkogrod.

CHAPTER SEVEN

Ullanor – primary landing zones

The crack of detonating missiles announced the arrival of the Black Templars. Lascannon beams and the bark of autocannons greeted the orks that scurried from their ugly barrack blocks, heading towards a ring of improvised anti-aircraft emplacements set about the edge of the huge crater.

Three Storm Eagles descended, weapons scouring the aliens and buildings scattered on the waste ground surrounding the flat expanse. Above them a pair of Thunderhawk transporters swooped groundwards, each bearing a Predator tank in its grip.

Thick dust and ash swirled as retro-thrusters fired, slowing the Thunderhawks over the last few metres of their landing. Before the extended hydraulic legs had touched down the assault ramps opened, spewing forth the warriors of Bohemond.

The High Marshal bounded forward, every leap covering two dozen metres with the aid of bursts from his jump pack. His honour guard followed a few metres behind, chainswords whirring.

Other squads fanned out across the crater, their bolters snapping as they gunned down greenskins skulking in the cover of revetments and trenches dug into the crater wall – fortifications that were poorly positioned, directed outwards to protect the crater.

Their warrior cargo disgorged, the Storm Eagles lifted off in a fresh gale of grit and flame, their renewed storm of fire levelling several more bunkers and hovels. The transporters took their place, dropping their battle tanks, tracks already spinning, the last couple of metres. As the Predators landed they lurched forward in spumes of dust, turret and sponson locks disengaging to allow their gunners to open fire. Heavy bolter rounds and concentrated autocannon salvoes added to the storm of destruction tearing along the crater walls.

Bohemond's squad reached the incline just as a hellstrike missile streaked overhead to pierce an armoured gun turret turning in their direction. The detonation tore the emplacement apart from within, scattering burning metal and charred ork flesh over the bare rock of the crater edge.

The High Marshal's jump pack easily took him over a chest-high retaining wall. Plunging into the trench beyond, he landed on a greenskin, the impact shattering its skull beneath his armoured boots even as his sword cleaved through the neck of another.

The rest of his honoured veterans crashed into the fortifications, hewing through the aliens within. Snarling greenskins and black-armoured warriors turned the entrenchment into a boiling melee while more blasts and bolts screamed overhead.

It took twenty seconds to clear the first stretch of trenchline.

'Is that the best these scum can offer?' roared Eddarin. The sergeant tore the head from an ork corpse and with a snarl threw it at the burning fortifications further up the slope. 'We came seeking warriors and found juveniles and cripples!'

Bohemond saw that it was true. Most of the bodies were of smaller greenskins, poorly armoured and armed. The few that seemed to have attained mature size and weight sported prosthetics and bionics, some so crude as to be simple hooks and plain metal peg legs.

'Gun garrison, poor duty for an ork,' said Bohemond.

'Such is the number plaguing the Segmentum Solar, perhaps all of their true warriors have deserted this waste-hole,' said Eddarin, sounding disappointed by the prospect.

Bohemond pointed with his sword to the building-covered mountain reaching over the horizon, the city obscured by distance and the shimmer of its force field.

'Foes enough await our righteous intentions, brothers,' said the High Marshal. 'The Great Beast lurks within that city and with the Emperor as my witness I declare the abomination will fall to the blade of a Black Templar. As Sigismund upon the bloodied fields of Terra, so we shall seek out the strongest foes and overcome them.'

He moved his blade towards the sky, where the black dots of descending drop pods were visible against the low clouds. With them emerged bulkier shapes, more Thunderhawk transporters laden with Rhino armoured carriers and other vehicles.

'We push on to Gorkogrod, High Marshal?' asked Eddarin, moving to the edge of the trench.

'Not yet. Temper your zeal, brother-sergeant,' replied Bohemond. 'We hold the landing zone until our allies in the Navy have deposited the regiments of the Astra Militarum. We are the sharp spearpoint, but the weight of the haft must follow us today.'

Eddarin looked up at the crater's edge and Bohemond could imagine his sergeant's desire to continue the attack, his longing to take the fight to the enemy and punish them for their innumerable transgressions against the Emperor.

'Justice will be done, brothers, vengeance will be served,' he assured his warriors. He gestured towards the remaining buildings. 'Ensure nothing lives that does not call the Emperor master.'

Bohemond activated his jump pack and bounded from the trench, angling towards the burning buildings ahead. Around the crater, black-armoured warriors pushed through the fire and ruin.

'The highway is secure, Lord Commander.' Odaenathus used the high-powered vox-unit of his Land Raider command tank to transmit his report. Even though only fifteen kilometres separated him from Koorland's position, the vox-breaking interference reduced the range of his war-plate's communicator to a few hundred metres. Contact with orbit was virtually non-existent.

'Astra Militarum landings are progressing on schedule,'

he continued. 'Armoured, artillery and infantry companies are awaiting our advance.'

'Understood, Chapter Master,' came Koorland's crackle-broken reply. 'You are authorised to conduct the second phase. Companies from Issachar's command will rendez-vous at the primaris target grid in three hours.'

'Affirmative, Lord Commander.'

Odaenathus shut down the transmitter and replaced his helmet. Pushing open the upper hatch of the Land Raider, he climbed out onto the roof to survey the unfolding scene.

The Ultramarines were a cordon of blue describing an arc nearly two kilometres long, a wall of armoured warriors between the landing zone and Gorkogrod some twenty kilometres away. His auto-senses picked up the faint bark of bolters as squads continued to clear the surrounding wasteland of xenos. Thunderhawks, Whirlwind missile launchers and Land Speeders were extending the Ultramarines' perimeter, pounding alien fortifications, weakening them in preparation for the armoured assault of Predators, Vindicators and Land Raiders that Odaenathus would lead. Overhead roared Imperial Navy bombers, destined for targets further along the main arterial route into the ork city.

There seemed little response from the orks. Considering a large enemy force had landed within striking distance of their capital, the counter-offensive by the greenskins had been minimal. Lacklustre. All that the Ultramarines commander knew of the greenskins told him that they were voracious fighters, lusting for battle. Even if some grander strategy was desired by the Great Beast, it seemed unlikely to overrule the base instincts of the orks in the immediate vicinity. The lack of response left Odaenathus feeling ill at ease, unable to test his theories but aware that all was not as it appeared.

Adeptus Mechanicus bulk servitors cleared the wreckage of the buildings turned to rubble by the Ultramarines' attack, ploughs and pneumatic shovels turning masonry, metal and dirt into earthworks for the Astra Militarum engineers to fortify while simultaneously clearing more landing zone for the next wave of transports.

Of the stronghold that had squatted on the ridge two hours earlier, only broken debris remained. Ork cadavers were treated like the rest of the waste, unceremoniously dumped into pits dug into the polluted earth, a task that had been assigned to the punishment platoons of the Astra Militarum landing forces. They laboured with scarves tied over their bare faces, sweating despite the chill of the uplands. Black-coated commissars watched them closely, never slow to shout admonishment at any that seemed to slacken in their labours.

Naval drop-ships formed an inner boundary, seventeen of them so far, as many again still arriving from orbit. Some were tank carriers, flat and broad, with wide doors that allowed their cargoes to disembark three abreast. The troop barges were longer and narrower, hundred-strong columns of infantry emerging at the double.

'A labour misspent, Brother Chapter Master.'

Odaenathus turned at the metallic growl of Ancient Selatonus. The Dreadnought approached from the right, the top of his armoured plates almost level with the roof of the Land Raider. Encased within the plasteel, ceramite and adamantium giant were the system-sustained bodily remnants of a Space Marine, a great hero from the battles of Calth-That-Was.

'Misspent, Venerable Brother?' Odaenathus reviewed his dispositions and could see nothing amiss. 'What labour goes awry?'

'Siege lines... Supply corridors... These are the works of an occupying force, Chapter Master,' the Dreadnought said, every word from his vocalisers heavy with artificially intoned gravitas. He raised a claw-tipped power fist and pointed towards the distant objective. 'We come to kill the Great Beast. Our sojourn here will not last long, in victory or defeat.'

Odaenathus thought about this for several seconds, reviewing the situation. It was a planetary landing on an unprecedented scale. There were protocols and doctrines to ensure all passed smoothly. He caught himself, realising the error of his logic. The landings were unprecedented by *his* experience, but for a veteran of the Heresy Wars they were a straightforward incursion.

'What counsel would you share, Ancient One?' he asked the Dreadnought.

'Speed in all things, Chapter Master. The Astra Militarum are capable of fending for themselves. We should strike for the city as soon as possible.'

The Chapter Master nodded and moved back to the hatch. He needed to request fresh orders from the Lord Commander.

From the observation platform of the *Praetor Fidelis*, Field-Legatus Otho Dorr could more clearly see the odd topography of the landing zone. From orbit it had looked like a series of eight mesas, each rising a few hundred metres from the wastelands' mean level. On the upper gallery of his Capitol Imperialis command vehicle, itself forty metres high, the regularity, the sheer flatness of the surrounding rocky plateaus, struck him as conspicuous.

The immense war engine rumbled on, its tracks leaving metre-deep trails of compacted ash and dust. Around the *Praetor Fidelis* smaller tanks and assault gun squadrons moved away from the landers, following the command vehicle like the tail of a comet. Sentinel walkers and Rough Rider companies moved ahead to scout the best route for the *Praetor Fidelis* and more super-heavy tanks descending in the next wave.

A sudden vibration silenced the chatter of vox-operators and junior officers. Dorr felt the movement again, a shift in the ground significant enough that it could be felt through the grinding of the Capitol Imperialis' tracks and the constant rumble of its engines.

'Galtan!' His staff lieutenant snapped to attention at the sound of his name. 'What was that? Contact the tech-priests immediately. I want...'

The next tremor caused the lumen fittings to sway from the ceiling. Several of the deck's occupants had to grab their consoles to stop themselves tipping from their stools. Dorr swayed with the movement, stumbling as he took a step towards the reinforced windows.

Looking down he saw that several of the surrounding vehicles had bogged down, caught as shifting dunes slid into newly formed dells littering the canyons between the plateaus.

'Sir, look at the rock faces!'

Galtan's call drew the field-legatus' gaze to the cliff a few hundred metres directly ahead of the *Praetor Fidelis*. Boulders tumbled in a shower of dust. Through the murk of the landslide he saw racks run up the length of the rock. Stone split along unseen fault lines, thousands of tonnes of rock shearing away as something beneath – within – moved.

Alarm sirens shrieked from half a dozen positions as the ground lurched again, tipping the Capitol Imperialis to the left. Men and women tumbled across the observation deck and mechanical howls of protests shuddered through the war machine as drive systems tried to continue pushing the tilting *Praetor Fidelis* into the growing drifts of rock, sand and ash.

'All drives to idle!' barked Dorr.

'Sir...' Galtan's hand tugged at the field-legatus' brocaded sleeve. 'You have to come to the gyro. I've ordered full staff council evacuation.'

'You've ordered...?'

'My prerogative, field-legatus.' The junior officer signalled to a stern-faced commissar standing by the stairwell that led up to the flight platform atop the command vehicle. 'Strechan will look after you.'

'Come with me, sir.' Strechan's tone suggested he would brook no argument. His hand on the butt of a shock maul indicated he was also willing to take physical measures to ensure the field-legatus' safety.

Dorr allowed himself to be hurried up the stairs. Emerging onto the flight platform he saw that the Capitol Imperialis had heeled over almost twenty degrees. The recon gyro – a

four-rotored flyer capable of carrying five men in addition
to the pilot – was still tightly gripped by landing claws.

'What is happening?' Dorr demanded, stepping away
from the gaggle of officers surging up the stairs behind him.

Strechan looked as though he might intervene but stopped
as the field-legatus directed a glare at him.

'You may have the authority to detain me, commissar, but
I would think twice about exercising it.'

The towering rock plateaus were falling to pieces, revealing glinting metal beneath. Like petals unfolding, huge
plates hinged down, unleashing crushing deluges of rock
onto the men and tanks between. Looking behind, Dorr
could see one of the massive structures fully opened. Where
there had been a mesa of solid stone – so he had thought
– he could see a pointed dome at least a hundred metres
across. It was painted in huge checks of red and black.

'Is that...?'

'Yessir,' Galtan said hurriedly, seizing hold of the stunned
field-legatus' belt to drag him towards the open doors of
the gyro. The blades started to spin, the whine of motors
almost lost under the tumult of falling rocks and the shrieks
of pulverised tank armour. The cacophony swallowed the
screams of the dying, their last cries passing unheard forty
metres below.

Bundled into the gyro, Dorr had not even strapped on
his safety harness when the engines pitched to a shriek
and he felt the craft lift away. Already at an awkward angle,
the gyro sheared sideways towards the grey-and-black ava-
lanche, until the pilot heaved the flyer into a swift climb. A
cloud of choking ash and dust mixed with exhaust smoke

swept through the still-open door of the compartment, coating uniforms, lips and skin with powdery residue. The updraught shook the gyro, its rotors rattling through stone splinters.

The field-legatus shouldered past Galtan, noting that Commissar Strechan had remained behind on the stricken Capitol Imperialis. Through the murk, wiping grit from his eyes, Dorr looked out of the ascending gyro, able to see across the expanse of the landing zone.

He could not credit his own senses at first, but the impossible forced its way into recognition. Where there had been rock and wilderness, now Dorr watched eight missiles push up from their silos, each defying sanity with their size.

'We have to warn the others,' he croaked, swallowing dust. A captain manning the vox-station looked at him, the blood drained from his face. He was holding the speaker-piece against his ear to listen over the continuing storm of noise.

'They already know, sir. By the Throne, they already know...'

Like a cornered animal, Ullanor bared its fangs.

Years of psychodoctrination meant that Captain Valefor could not panic. Vigorous mental conditioning and genetic therapy had eliminated biological fear. Even so, as a cocktail of hormones and stimulants raced through his bloodstream, as twin hearts thundered into accelerated life and his tertiary lung inflated to flood his system with oxygen, the biological call to action that seared through his body and thoughts came very close.

The desert had swallowed six Astra Militarum drop-craft already, the yawning chasm that had split the basin still widening. Dust and ash flowed like water into the breach, dragging tanks and men with it. Ruddy light, the gleam of the abyss itself, burned from the new crevasse, and with it came an ear-piercing screech of tortured metal.

The plain was shifting under his feet, toppling columns of soldiers that had been advancing from the landing barges. He could feel himself moving slowly to the right without taking a step. He watched as a Leman Russ tank tilted, trapped against a boulder. Hatches slammed open as the crew tried to scramble to safety. Too late, too slow, they fell into the gaping rift with their vehicle.

The vox was a thrum of meaningless noise, every general channel and frequency overloaded. He shut down all but the Adeptus Astartes feeds. The garbled bursts were replaced by clipped, efficient reports and unruffled commands. The relative quiet allowed him to focus on the immediate situation.

Valefor's auto-senses brought to him the insistent bellows of officers and the terrified shouts of dying Guardsmen. Many of the Astra Militarum infantry were breaking ranks, fleeing towards the distant lip of the basin. Commissars did their best to prevent the retreat becoming a rout – the Blood Angel could hear them exhorting their men to keep weapons and packs, ordering them to drag their heavy bolters and lascannons, autocannons and mortars through the undulating dunes of ash and dirt.

A slew of rocks and earth was building up against the walls of the hollow, forming a ramp for some of the vehicles to drive over while men clambered through the churning debris. Many disappeared beneath the surface, while others were bloodily crushed by rolling boulders or suffocated by erupting clouds of dust.

'Our forces are clear, captain.' Marbas was at Valefor's shoulder, golden armour coated with dark grey ash. He waved a hand towards red-liveried Rhinos, Predators and Land Raiders just visible through the whirling dust-storm. 'What are your orders?'

Valefor could see that the chasm was now nearly fifty metres wide. Several of his Land Speeder crews had already taken it upon themselves to act as lifeboats, skimming dangerously close to the rolling stones and earth, laden with Guardsmen clinging to every handhold. Valkyries and Vendettas in the colours of the Imperial Navy and the Coltain XV Air Dragoons skimmed to and fro, their hoverjets kicking up even more ash and soot. The men and women aboard hauled up as many fellow soldiers as they could, filling their troop compartments to bursting. Here and there brave pilots set their machines down so that wounded soldiers could be loaded aboard. Valefor saw a Vendetta crushed like a rations can as a boulder twice the size of a troop transport tumbled into it.

'Get the Thunderhawks, rapid evacuation.' Valefor watched as a ring of drop pods vanished into the depths. He had landed in one just a few hours earlier.

He turned and waded back down into the basin. His auto-senses flickered through various modes until they settled on thermal, picking out the fleeing men and women like flares at night. A gaggle of soldiers struggled towards him a few metres away. The swirling ash was like quicksand, dissolving underfoot. Valefor heaved the closest man out of the mire as easily as an adult lifts a child, almost throwing him towards the basin's edge. Another cradled a broken arm, blood staining his light blue uniform.

Valefor saw the injury and knew that the soldier would not fight again. He stepped past, ignoring the man's pleas for help. Other Blood Angels followed, advancing into the raging storm to help the beleaguered Imperial Guardsmen.

'Concentrate on the uninjured,' Valefor voxed to his companions. The mounting dirt was heaped up almost to his knees. The captain kicked himself free and looked around at the devastation. From the long-range broadcasts on the vox he knew that their predicament was far from unique. 'We're going to need every able-bodied soldier.'

CHAPTER EIGHT

Ullanor – low orbit

Once more, dear friend, once more. Now is the moment.

Nearly all of the Cult Mechanicus personnel were already on Ullanor or in atmospheric transit. Aboard the *Cortix Verdana* the eruption of surface defence systems burst across the sensors as a stream of alerts and surveyor spikes. With two-thirds of his divisible consciousness plugged directly into the assessor arrays to monitor the ongoing landings, Gerg Zhokuv felt it like a burning sensation racing through his being.

'It is... astounding,' said Laurentis, gazing at the images arranged on the visual displays. Hundreds of installations appeared, massive thermal plumes and energy signatures like celebration lights flickering on the screens. Around the cities the force fields gleamed, encompassing entire settlements. 'Not an attack moon. An attack *planet*?'

'Thousands of soldiers are dying,' Delthrak snapped in response to his fellow tech-priest's enthusiasm. 'Our assault is crumbling before our eyes.'

The surge of signals from orbital and ground-based data-feeds crackled lightning-like through Zhokuv's synapses, the equivalent to a blinding, deafening pulse. They emerged in a wave from a battery of outposts almost directly below the Martian ship's orbital arc.

'We are being targeted!' the dominus roared across the vocal and sub-aural channels of the war-forge.

'By what?' inquired Delthrak, tapping into the data-stream.

Zhokuv did not have to reply.

His subconscious reaction directed power to the main void shield generators and shut down reactor plasma inlets as he braced the starship for the inevitable attack. Anti-torpedo las weapons thrummed into life, though they were of virtually no use against surface-launched missiles. The targeting arrays would not have time to adjust in the moments between the projectiles breaking atmosphere and striking the ship in low orbit. Damage teams and repair servitors were despatched to their emergency positions while the more vulnerable parts of the ship were evacuated completely except for servitor personnel.

A vessel the size of the *Cortix Verdana* had no chance of evading the incoming attack. Instead, the ship assumed its maximum defensive posture, the equivalent of curling into a foetal ball and awaiting the worst.

They did not have to wait long.

Less than a minute after detecting the first defence activations, Zhokuv sensed a ripple of energetic particles erupting from one of the ground installations. In less than a second the beam struck the *Cortix Verdana*.

'Gravitic attack!' The warning raced through the ship's

systems. Klaxons blared. Those that could made fast to whatever they could hold.

The wave of anti-gravitic energy passed through the void shields without effect. It slammed into the planetwards decks, instantly crumpling metres-thick armour, tearing chunks of plasteel and adamantium from their housings.

The physical damage was significant, but worse still, the beam ruptured the basic fabric of the gravity well, dragging the ship towards Ullanor. The sudden acceleration created a form of weightlessness on board, overpowering even the artificial gravity. Personnel and equipment were sent flying from the decks, slamming into ceilings and bulkheads as though caught on an aircraft in horrendous turbulence. Zhokuv felt pressure doors bursting and vacuum seals shredding under the immense forces.

The dominus knew from all previous reports that even the massive engines of the *Cortix Verdana* could not resist the power of the gravity beam. Instead he diverted all remaining energy to the physical defences and energy shields.

'Atmospheric entry in thirty seconds,' groaned an alarm-servitor.

The strategium was a scene of chaos, tech-priests and servitors thrown like dolls as another wave of impossible gravitic energy flared along the *Cortix Verdana*. Zhokuv had no time to spare for the broken bodies littering the deck – every navigational shield and altitude jet burst into life at his command, easing the massive starship into a better angle of entry.

Even so, the flare of frictional heat from the thickening atmosphere overloaded the ship's sensors. Blinded, the

flagship of the Adeptus Mechanicus plunged into Ullanor's skies.

'Launch everything!' bellowed Koorland. 'Anything that can drop, get it off the ships. Any vessel that has already despatched must break orbit immediately.'

Thane was already barking commands at the vox-officer, demanding reports from the surface. Warning alerts wailed into life as the *Alcazar Remembered* took evasive action. The battle-barge fired its main engines, heading towards Ullanor in an attempt to break the target lock that had overloaded its surveyor systems a minute earlier.

'Incoming missiles,' growled Thane from a monitor station. 'A dozen at least.'

The flat areas chosen as landing grounds by their forces had in fact been the covers to immense silos of anti-ship guns and missiles. Not just physical missiles targeted the orbiting fleets – powerful gravitic manipulators were turning ships inside out, pulling them down to fiery deaths in the atmosphere or tossing them into deep space. Strangely pulsating green rays sliced warships in two while cluster-missiles engulfed descending drop-ships with thousands of detonations, and rapid-firing flak guns smashed apart plummeting drop pods.

'We can't stay here,' snarled Koorland. He started towards the door of the command bridge. 'Alert all combat personnel to prepare for launch. Drop pods and Thunderhawks.'

'We're evacuating, Lord Commander?'

'Attacking, while we can.'

'And Lord Vulkan?' asked Thane, following his Lord Commander. The remaining Space Marines left their positions, their roles handed to unaugmented officers and servitors. Fists Exemplar across the ship would be doing the same. Every warrior ready for combat would be at his drop-station in minutes.

'I will speak with him myself,' said Koorland. He took his helmet from his belt as the doors wheezed open. With a last look at Thane he fitted the helm.

'Brace for impact.' The mechanical tones of the alert servitor across the shipwide vox did nothing to convey the urgency of its message. 'Impact imminent.'

Koorland grabbed a bulkhead, pressing close to the plasteel. The others found similar handholds and waited.

Three seconds later the ork missiles erupted around the battle-barge in a storm of fire and metal. Void shields flared black and blue, warp-shunting what they could before their generators overloaded, exploding with showers of sparks in the bowels of the ship.

The *Alcazar Remembered* shook from prow to stern as the remaining energy and debris slammed into its starboard side. The entire ship lurched. Lights flickered. Koorland felt as much as heard the rip of tortured metal shuddering along the length of the battle-barge.

Damage reports flowed through the vox but he cut them off and signalled the quarters of the primarch. Unlike before, Vulkan responded immediately.

'The orks have woken up,' said the primarch.

'A quarter of the fleet is already in ruins, my lord,' replied

Koorland. He hit the call rune for the conveyor and chains rattled in the shaft beyond the heavy doors. 'They hit us exactly when we could do the least about it, mid-drop.'

'And your strategy, Lord Commander?'

'We have to complete the drop, Lord Vulkan. Our ships cannot stay in orbit and survive.'

'The army will be stranded on Ullanor.' Koorland heard the grinding noise of the primarch's chamber doors across the link. 'While these weapons remain active there can be no return from the surface.'

'That does not concern us, does it?' Koorland said. The conveyor arrived and he wrenched open the door. He and the others crowded into the cage within. Thane operated the controls, taking them down to the launch decks.

Memories crammed into Koorland's thoughts as tightly as the warriors in the conveyor. Of Ardamantua. His brothers penned in, dying by the score with no escape. The buzz of suppressed vox-traffic reminded him of the confused warnings and alerts of that dreadful day.

'Lord Commander?' Vulkan had been speaking. 'Koorland, respond.'

'It is of no concern,' the Imperial Fist said, pushing back any thoughts of his Chapter's demise. 'The orks were ready, no matter what. The dilemma has not changed. Attack, or return to Terra. We came to Ullanor with a single purpose. That mission remains. The Beast must die!'

Bohemond watched with mounting incredulity as the barrels of three immense cannons emerged from the splitting crater. Secondary guns broke free of rock cladding in the surrounding hills. Within seconds they opened fire, spewing a torrent of exploding shells and pulsing blasts into the drop-ships bringing down the Astra Militarum forces.

He looked up into the sky and saw drop-craft burning, falling like meteors. Showers of debris rained down, some pieces as large as battle tanks. Charred skeletons and bloody body parts fell too, striking terror into the squads of Guardsmen fleeing the carnage.

The main cannons boomed into life. Bohemond's auto-senses blotted out the ear-shattering noise but the shockwave threw hundreds of Astra Militarum fighters to the ground, screaming as their eardrums burst. The wave swept onwards, tipping armoured vehicles and sending Land Speeders and Navy aircraft into mad spins. Bohemond's armour registered the wash of pressure over him with a row of amber warning sigils.

The High Marshal could just about track the supersonic course of the shells towards orbit but in moments they were lost in the high cloud. His eye was drawn to the upper reaches, his disbelief increased. A scarlet comet fell, larger than anything he had ever seen. Increasing the resolution of his auto-senses, he magnified the view.

The descending ship was wreathed in fire, trailing broken plates and corpses like smoke. In general shape it was an inverted pyramid, a stepped ziggurat of many levels. He could see the blazons of the Adeptus Mechanicus in many places and realised it was the flagship of the dominus.

Despite its calamitous fall, the ship was not without control. Bohemond could see that its trajectory was flattening

sharply, some mechanism of the Cult Mechanicus lessening the speed and incline of its course. Distance and size made its rapid descent seem almost stately.

The *Cortix Verdana* hit the ground many kilometres away, just beyond the horizon. The ork cannons fired again even as a bright flash of detonating plasma lit the distant sky.

Bohemond turned away from the fallen ship and voxed his warriors.

'The xenos have hidden their holes well, my brothers. Now they are revealed and our vengeance will be swift.' He activated his jump pack and bounded back towards the crater. 'In attacking, they have left themselves vulnerable. Into the breach they have opened! Destroy the guns! Praise those that slay in the Emperor's name!'

Esad Wire, known to a few by the title of Beast Krule, let the body of the greenskin slip to the ground, its throat crushed. His synskin suit was hidden beneath a few scraps of clothes and armour he had looted from other targets. The silhouette they gave him was more of a disguise than the shifting cameleoline, though he could not hope to look like an ork. He had smeared a little of their filthy blood and spoor over himself to cover his own scent, having been briefed on orks from the Officio Assassinorum's mission data repositories. Despite its limits, his rough silhouette had confused the greenskins he had encountered long enough to get in range with weighted fists or needle pistol.

Grand Master Vangorich had expressed the uniqueness of the mission – rarely was an operative of the Assassins despatched to slay a non-human target. Their purview was far more concentrated on the rogues and rebellions within the Imperium.

In fact there was almost nothing about the orks at all in the archives, and Vangorich had drawn in favours from the Inquisition to supplement their records.

Krule stepped over a corpse, past two other dead orks that had been lounging by their armoured wagon. The complacency of the aliens – the sheer casualness they showed in the face of a massed human attack – worried him as he pulled himself up into the driver's position. Settling into the bucket seat, he looked over the crude pedals and controls, working out where throttle and gearing systems were located.

He heard a dull, distant thunder that he instantly recognised as the retort of a large cannon. It continued for some time, many guns firing not quite in unison. He waited to hear the corresponding explosions in the city but nothing came, yet the fusillade continued.

Perplexed, he stood up, the better to see over the corrugated iron and broken plastek rookeries of the ork shanty piled up on the foot of the mountain that was Gorkogrod. The haze of the force dome gave everything beyond the city's borders a greenish cast. Streaks of shells disappeared into the cloud. Looking left and right the Assassin saw the flashes of other weapons – beams and blasts and oscillating green waves from emplacements somewhere beyond the city's semi-derelict outskirts.

He had seen drop-ships descending all afternoon, accompanied by the occasional shower of artificial meteors when the Adeptus Astartes had made secondary drops.

The Assassin had paid it no mind. He had been expecting floods of alien warriors to pour from Gorkogrod to fend off the attacks, and had hoped to use such activity and confusion to slip through the ork city. Now the lack of response from the orks was explained. He had seen no defences as he had brought his commandeered aircraft down, but could see that the firepower being unleashed into the sky and towards orbit was devastating.

Dropping down into the seat, Krule started the engine. Its throaty roar accompanied a cough of oily smoke from the pierced exhausts flanking the machine. He slammed his foot onto the throttle pedal and sped out of the courtyard and into the street beyond, crashing through a crowd of greenskins that had emerged from their hovels to stare at the anti-orbital attacks. One bounced from the large iron buffer on the front of the battlewagon; another went jolting under a wheel.

Ignoring their death-cries, Krule powered the vehicle uphill, heading as fast as he could towards the inner city.

CHAPTER NINE

Ullanor – Gorkogrod

I dared what others could not. I knew what awaited me in the inferno and I stepped willingly into the flames. No other could. As above, so below, the fight without and the battle within. Endless torment, unending perseverance. Not one of my brothers could have done it, in body or in mind. It was my agony alone to suffer.

For what? For maggots to erupt from the corpse of greatness, devouring blindly the very thing that sustains them, consuming all until is spent. The Imperium is a husk; even the rot has eaten itself.

The city was ringed with fire. Devastation caused by crashing ships and burning debris spread far into the wastelands that surrounded the ork capital – wastelands that had not been empty of life, but concealed a profusion of orks beneath rock and ash.

'Be thankful for small boons,' said Vulkan. Thane looked from the Thunderhawk at the fires and wreckage. The primarch spoke from the main compartment, making the already over-filled space even smaller with his bulk. Thirty-five more Space Marines had managed to fit into a space intended for thirty, even with the primarch. Similarly laden, every drop pod, gunship and shuttle on the *Alcazar Remembered* had been despatched within minutes of the first ork attack.

'Small boons, lord primarch?' asked the Fists Exemplar Chapter Master.

'Our fall from grace has killed no small number of orks as well.'

'Forgive me, my lord, for taking little comfort in that fact.' Thane activated the powerful vox of the Thunderhawk to contact his battle-barge. The signal was surprisingly clear when Shipmaster Weylon Kale responded. Evidently much of the vox-clutter had been deliberately created by the orks to mask their anti-orbit weapons.

'Substantial damage, Chapter Master,' Kale reported in response to Thane's inquiry. 'But we have attained higher orbit. It seems that the initial attack was a massive drain on the power grid of Ullanor and their targeting systems are having trouble tracking us at this distance.'

'How much of the fleet has survived?' asked the Lord Commander, sat next to Thane.

'Half of the warships, barely any transports. We are also detecting increased activity from the ork vessels in the system. It seems they will try to pick over the scraps. Admiral Acharya has taken command for the Imperial Navy. He assured me that they can cope with the void threat for the time being.'

'Low orbit is out of the question,' said Thane. 'We cannot risk any more ships even for the benefit of orbital firepower.'

'Agreed,' said Koorland. 'We have perhaps one more opportunity to strike with everything – we cannot waste it.'

'You have a strategy, Lord Commander?' Vulkan shifted his bulk and looked through the door into the command deck.

'I do, Lord Vulkan. What I said before still holds true. We must attack as swiftly as possible. Our mission has become threefold. We must determine the exact location of the Beast for an overwhelming concentration of force. We cannot be tricked into thinking a whole world is arrayed against us. It will take time for the orks to mobilise any force of note from the other cities and move them to our battlezone. We must use what strength we can to break into Gorkogrod and destroy the Great Beast before we are overwhelmed.

'In order to do that we must first disable the force fields and weapons protecting the city against orbital support. Also, we need to disrupt the gathering ork armies so that both of the previous objectives can be achieved before the massive weight of ork numbers can be brought to bear.'

Vulkan nodded his approval.

'A sure course of action, Lord Commander. The warriors of the Adeptus Astartes must bear the brunt of the assault on the city. As much as it seems counter to your ethos, I would spare the Chapters the brunt of the fighting before then.'

'I can think of several commanders that will not like the idea of holding back,' said Koorland.

'Bohemond, for one,' said Thane. 'And there will be others of similar thought. Those that supported his pre-emptive strike spring to mind.'

'What happened was unavoidable,' Koorland replied, staring out of the canopy. Night was falling, the darkness lit by plasma fires and the occasional jade glow of defence beams and scarlet of missile trails, the sunset obscured by columns of black smoke. 'Whether today or tomorrow or the day after, we would have landed and the orks would have revealed their intent. Perhaps the High Marshal's attack was not so rash. Had the orks had time to prepare even further for our landings we might not have the period of relative grace we have now. There has been little sign of enemy movement on the ground to exploit our predicament.'

'Why?' said Vulkan. 'The city must house thousands of orks. Why has the Great Beast not unleashed its horde on our remnants before we can gather ourselves?'

'I feel that you know the answer to that already, Lord Vulkan,' said Thane.

Koorland shook his head.

'The Great Beast does not need to strike. It knows that we come for it. We do not face a childish mind, but a calculating leader. It will let us bleed ourselves on the walls of its fortresses before it wipes the remains from the planet.'

'That fails to comfort me, too,' said Thane.

'Which is why we cannot expend our best,' Koorland said quietly, looking at Vulkan. 'Dross and slaves may man the defences, but their guns will slay Space Marines as surely as they will combat servitors and Astra Militarum.'

'It is not the place of the Adeptus Astartes to hide behind the shields of others,' said Thane, not believing the strategy his superiors discussed.

'Nor shall they,' said Vulkan. 'If Bohemond wishes to be

the point of the spear, let him. Guardsmen and skitarii will not breach the city, but the Black Templars might. Lord Commander, I appreciate the sentiment but you mistake the intent of my words. We cannot fight a war of attrition. We must trust to others to guard our backs while we turn every thought to piercing Gorkogrod.'

'Very well, lord primarch. The Astra Militarum and the Cult Mechanicus will provide the weight behind our shaft. The Adeptus Astartes shall dare the ire of the orks.'

Koorland spoke with certainty, but Thane could not tell if it was simply the habit of the commander or genuine confidence. As the Thunderhawk touched down among the broken and burning remains of the fleet, he felt no particular reason to be hopeful.

'Let it not be said that we were found wanting when the Lord Commander called upon us!'

Vox-casters across the warzone relayed the field-legatus' words to his devastated, demoralised regiments. It was all he could do to summon the spirit to address them, ensconced just below the main turret of his new command vehicle: the *Dorn's Ire*, a Baneblade-class super-heavy tank. He considered the naming of the tank a good omen, but he knew there were those in his staff that thought otherwise. Of late, the legacy of the Imperial Fists primarch had suffered in reputation.

'Our goal is clear, our resolve unbroken,' he continued. He looked at one of the displays carrying a visual from the external pict-feeds. Ahead of the Baneblade, columns of tanks forced their way through the smashed remains of the

city outskirts. Chimera infantry fighting vehicles carrying armoured squads followed, ready to deploy their platoons in support of the battle tanks. 'We are to be the shield to the Space Marines, the rear guard that will allow them to be the blade that prises open the defences of the city, so that all of us can bring the battle directly to the Great Beast.'

Artillery batteries of hastily mustered multiple rocket launchers and self-propelled guns started to lay down a barrage of fire across the line of advance. Manticores launched their hail of missiles into the ruins while Basilisks pounded out shell after shell, flattening any building left standing by the rain of destruction that had fallen from orbit. Daring radioactive fire, companies from the Elran Fourth Pioneer Corps had salvaged a trio of Deathstrike launchers from their drop-carriers, but Dorr was conserving their deadly vortex warheads for the time being.

The bombardment was fierce, but nothing like the tempest of shell and rocket he might have hoped to unleash had his force landed intact. But big guns would not win this war. The initial reports from rocket and bombing attacks by Imperial Navy Marauders suggested that the power shields protecting Gorkogrod would be as impervious to ground-based weapons as they were to aerial and orbital attacks. Such information had been paid for by the lives of the air crews, shot down by an iron ring of anti-air defences around the outskirts of the ork city. Even this showed the depth of cunning of the Great Beast, having remained dormant long enough to allow the Adeptus Mechanicus flights to approach and to draw the attack of the Emperor's servants.

As was almost universally true, it would require soldiers on the ground to force their way into the city. That was the purpose of the Astra Militarum. Given how many had already died it seemed likely that none of his brave Imperial Guard would leave Ullanor. A less experienced commander might have given his soldiers hope and allayed their fears. Dorr knew better. He knew that any soldier of the Imperium worth the name, any true servant of the Emperor that had passed through the firestorm unleashed against them, cared nothing for survival now. Whether for themselves or worlds lost or dead comrades, the Astra Militarum would fight to punish the orks and give their lives in the effort. The commissars reported barely any desertions despite the disaster that had beset the landings.

Dorr was not surprised. Even for those of low resolve, where was there to run? The only option was to fight as hard as possible to survive.

The majority of the foe came in savage mobs of infantry, emerging from massive fortifications of which the surface bastions and citadels had been but the tip of the iceberg. Hundreds of kilometres of city extended beneath the ash dunes. Much of it had been collapsed by fallen starships, but a maze of tunnels and chambers remained, populated by hordes of greenskins ready to burst free almost anywhere.

The main battle cannon of the *Dorn's Ire* thundered into life, hurling its massive shell into a building flanking the line of advance. Its lascannon sub-turrets spat white flares while heavy bolter sponsons sent out an almost constant stream of fire at the alien brutes skulking in the ruins.

The bulk of the army advanced on foot, keeping pace

with the broad-sided Baneblades, Stormblades and other super-heavies. Lasguns strobed red beams through the clouds of dust and grit while ork slug-throwers and energy weapons flared in reply. Scout teams in camouflaged fatigues surged ahead, their bayonets at the ready. Behind, smartly-uniformed troopers advanced in rank beneath fluttering standards and Imperial aquilas, defiant in the face of the orks' weapons.

Sentinel scout walkers stalked the ruins, their multi-lasers and autocannons picking out scattered groups of greenskins. In return, xenos tank-hunters sowed deadly anti-vehicle mines and lay in wait with short-ranged but powerful rocket launchers. Ork nobles twice the size of any unaugmented human led counter-charges with blazing-headed axes and growling chain weapons. They led hundreds of orks in bloody close assaults to cut down the servants of the Emperor by the score, before the fire of surviving Guardsmen slew them or drove them back into their holes.

Bulky-suited Deltronis fire teams with heavy flamers accompanied pairs of Hellhound flamethrower tanks, burning the greenskins from their lairs. In turn they were supported by specialist tunnel fighters brought from the hive cities of Hermetica. These ex-hive gangers were barely civilised, regarded as savages by many of their fellow regiments, but in the close confines of the ork weapon-site tunnels their barbarity was an advantage, matching the orks for sheer viciousness if not size and strength.

Demolisher tanks and siege bombards advanced behind the outer cordon of Leman Russ tanks. Where the enemy massed in some bastion or bunker unbreached by the carpet bombing of the Navy and the rolling barrage of the artillery, the wall-breakers moved forward and unleashed their fortress-busting salvoes.

A whine of alarms brought Galtan and two subalterns into the chamber, ready to throw themselves on top of the field-legatus. A few seconds passed and then impacts rang on the Baneblade's hull – a pattering of detonations that spread from the engine blocks behind and passed directly along the entire tank. Galtan visibly flinched, eyeing the vaulting of the reinforced ceiling that held up the turret.

'What was that?' asked one of the junior officers.

'Strafing run,' said another.

'What happened to our anti-air guns? Where are those damned Navy interceptors?' Galtan moved towards the vox-panel, but Dorr stopped him with a raised hand.

'They are protecting the squads on the tip of the attack, lieutenant.' Dorr shooed the staff officer away with a wave of his hand. 'A place far more suitable than guarding this armoured behemoth, regardless of the rank of its crew. This is the closest you've been to a battle, isn't it, Galtan?'

'I have had the privilege of serving on the command staff of three general-rank officers, field-legatus.'

'From a Capitol Imperialis or in orbit, yes?'

Galtan swallowed hard and examined his fingernails.

'Yes, field-legatus.'

'It is not an accusation,' Dorr assured him. 'I am certain you served with distinction. I do not claim any particular experience at close quarters myself. I earned my rank in the artillery regiments of Aldarast. Even so, it is important that we keep calm, no matter how hot things get around us.'

'I understand, sir.'

'I do have one suggestion though, lieutenant.'

'Sir?'

'There will be a time when the fighting gets close and dirty, when perhaps you and I even are required to remember our basic training and fire a weapon in anger. When that time comes, assure me of one thing, Galtan.'

'Anything, sir. My dedication will not fail, nor my courage.'

Dorr pointed to the empty holster at the lieutenant's hip.

'Remember to bring your laspistol.'

The strategium and inner chambers of the *Cortix Verdana* had been constructed as an armoured core, protected not only by a reinforced structure but also an onion-like, multi-layered field system. The central structure resembled the pyramid shape of the ship but on a much smaller scale, barely a hundred metres high, tilted at a sharp angle among a tattered cocoon of tangled cables, splintered walls and ruptured bulkheads. It was perhaps only due to these additional measures that Magos Laurentis was alive to loiter amongst the wreck of the war-forge with the other upper-hierarchy tech-priests, while the bulk of the ship and its crew lay scattered and burning over several square kilometres of devastated ork city.

A cadre of several hundred skitarii – the dominus' personal guard – held a perimeter just half a kilometre from where Laurentis watched the unfolding battle. Beyond them heavier engines of war waged their own fight – two Warlord Titans of the Legio Ultima had landed close to the crash site, another likely reason for Laurentis' continued mortal existence. The towering avatars of the Machine-God's wrath put forth an ear-splitting, blinding storm of fire from their immense rocket launchers, volcano cannon, turbolasers and macro-cannons, reducing clanking ork transports to careening piles of slag, obliterating mobs of aliens in blossoms of immolating fire.

Smaller war machines held the other approaches. Moving between the fume-wreathed remains of the engine decks and the glassy crater that had been a plasma reactor, a Warhound scout-class and two Reaver Battle Titans in the dark green and gold of the War Griffons supported maniples of red-armoured automaton warriors from the Legio Cybernetica. Any orks cunning, persistent or lucky enough to survive the ire of the Titans were hunted down by hulking mechanical brutes, targeted by raging bursts from incendine combustors or crushed with crackling power fists. Volkite blasts and the muzzle flash of macrostubbers added to the hellish glow of the flame-shrouded battle. Tracer rounds left actinic trails against a backdrop of the fading dusk while incendiary missiles burst in blooms of incandescent wrath.

The silhouette of a rare tri-legged Punisher-class Titan blocked out the sky above, standing guard over the upper ranks of Martian nobility with tezlan accelerators gleaming. The containment fields of its underslung plasma annihilator vibrated through the ground, and Laurentis' bionics, like a heartbeat.

Such protection did not render them immune to harm. Ork heavy guns had started shelling the Cult Mechanicus forces as they had assembled on the site of their fallen commanders. Stray rockets continued to sputter and spit past, detonating against the black metal of the war-forge's inner sanctum.

His recent near-fatal experiences had inured the magos to any anxiety concerning self-preservation, but he sensed the unease of his companions. He had no doubt that they would have preferred to stay within the armoured shell of the strategium block, but that was impossible. The glitter of las-cutters and corona of phase fields illuminated the interior as a full recovery phalanx attempted to free the dominus from the half-collapsed decks. Monotask servitors with cranes and heavy mechanical lifters pried apart the wreckage, red-robed tech-priests overseeing the oddly brutal-yet-delicate operation.

Delthrak's transmitter was a constant stream of coded orders, a rat-tat-tat barrage of signals that flitted through a sub-channel of Laurentis' auditory backups.

'Please stop that, it is impossible to think with the racket,' Laurentis told the Barbarian's Advocate. 'I am trying to metriculate.'

'Someone has to coordinate the defence while the dominus is discommoded,' replied Delthrak.

Laurentis could not see well after his most recent reconstruction, but from what he observed there was nothing to be done that wasn't already under way.

'I would also suggest that you cease distracting our line-commanders with this constant inanity,' the magos continued. 'They are far more experienced than you or I in these matters.'

'You have no rank here,' Delthrak snapped back. 'In fact, you have become utterly irrelevant.'

A particularly large and multicoloured explosion to their right drew everybody's attention. Just a few hundred metres away the red-armoured carapaces of several Kataphron warrior-constructs stood out starkly against the white ash and grey dust. Their weapons chattered, muzzle flare visible even at this distance when they engaged another foe, as yet out of sight past the scraps of the forge-ship littering the blasted hillsides. Until large numbers of infantry arrived, there would be gaps in the defensive enclosure – Titans were more properly suited to levelling cities than picking off infantry assaults.

A rocket whined overhead and crashed a few hundred metres away, behind the tech-priests. Another followed, striking closer. The deafening blast of a war-horn from the looming Punisher – the *Modus Destructor* – warned those below that it was moving. Skitarii squads scattered and the tech-priests moved closer to the inner shell as the gigantic construct stepped forward. The shell of an ork building collapsed under its clawed foot as the Titan settled in its new position.

Turning about its waist axis, the *Modus Destructor* brought its twin accelerators to bear on some target out of sight of Laurentis. A high-pitched wail split the air moments before the weapons lit up with a burst of azure light. Laurentis' inhuman sight picked up pulses of electromagnetic charge as a hail of hundreds of solid missiles flared into the darkness, shredding whatever engines or batteries had launched the rockets.

The magos caught a burst of vox-traffic emanating from the innards of the broken strategium. Tech-seers and servitors moved out of the structure, dragging twisted plates and carefully-sliced support struts with them.

'The dominus has been freed,' said Delthrak, decoding the data-stream microseconds before Laurentis. The Barbarian's Advocate's auto-synapses had not endured the turmoil that had battered Laurentis since he had been despatched to Ardamantua.

The cabal of ranking Cult Mechanicus huddled together as they approached the broad docking doors that had been freed by the work teams. Sputtering temporary lights lit the insides of the bay, casting an inconsistent crimson-and-amber gleam.

The deck floor shuddered, settling under a fresh weight, the crash of metal reverberating from the open hold. A large shadow eclipsed the internal light. A second later Dominus Zhokuv strode into view.

His pteknopic casing was hidden from view, located somewhere in the depths of the plates of armourplas, ceramite and plasteel. Twice as tall as a Space Marine Dreadnought, the dominus' war body hunched on dog-legs. Two volkite cannons flanked the central coffin housing Zhokuv's physical remains. Beneath this sarcophagus, field-sheathed power saws extended on articulated arms. A tangle of mechadendrites curled from under the carapace plates, tipped with a variety of appendages for fine motor work. The sparkle of an omnidirectional power shield caused the air to sputter with ionised particles, forcing the tech-priests back several paces as the giant walker emerged into the night. Two eye-like searchlamps sprang into life, bathing the assembled Cult Mechanicus with multi-spectral light.

'Praise the Machine-God!' Laurentis joined in with the hailed chorus, feeling an uncharacteristic surge of relief at the sight of the Cult Mechanicus commander. He reasoned it was simply the cessation of Delthrak's chatter that had ended his discomfort.

A burst of high-velocity data speared into Laurentis' cortical analysis cells, apprising him of the entire strategic situation in less than two seconds. Zhokuv had not been idle during his enforced absence, having assimilated the data-feeds of the remaining Adeptus Mechanicus assets and interfaced with the strategic and tactical systems of the Imperial Navy, Adeptus Astartes and Astra Militarum. It included every last detail until moments before his emergence, down to the level of individual squad auspex readings detected by the massive augur arrays of the war-forge. It was too much for Laurentis to comprehend as raw data, his afflicted brain instead summarising the mass of information in vaguely visual terms – a ring of green around the red runes of the Adeptus Mechanicus, while a black thunderbolt speared towards the ork city followed by a blue shield.

'The plan is simple, my learned companions,' the dominus boomed through his address systems. 'The Space Marines will seize approaches into the city interior. The Astra Militarum will hold the ground they take and shield them against counter-attack from the rear and flanks. Our task, blessed be the Omnissiah, is to locate and disable the anti-bombardment shield and anti-orbital weapons protecting Gorkogrod.'

'Would it not be better to spearhead the attack with our

Titans?' suggested Delthrak. Laurentis could not tell if he was simply fulfilling his role or expressing personal doubts.

In reply, the dominus remotely opened a specific data-packet in the cogitators of his minions. Laurentis reeled as the contents of the packet unfurled through his thoughts.

'Analysis of the ork brute-shield,' said Zhokuv. 'It combines the same energetic and gravitational properties as many of the grand weapons we have encountered previously, and those that assailed us in orbit, but utilised in a different fashion. Any void shield or power field we possess that contacts the ork brute-shield will detonate. We cannot send our engines through it with their fields deployed, and to do so without would see them destroyed in minutes by the orks within.'

'What if we cannot destroy the shield, dominus?' asked Delthrak.

'There is no retreat, no possible evacuation under present conditions. The Omnissiah will curse our existence and our infantry and vehicles will be forced to assault without Titan and orbital support.'

'They will die,' said Laurentis.

'Yes, they will. Which is why we must not fail. Mars demands success, even at the cost of our lives.'

Laurentis turned his attention from the dominus and focused on the mountain of lights that denoted the distant ork city, shimmering as though behind a heat haze. Lit from within by innumerable lamps and fires, studded with cannon-encrusted pinnacles and towers, Gorkogrod looked like a massive, squatting beast.

CHAPTER TEN

Ullanor – Gorkogrod, outer defences

*This again? It all resolves the same way, in blood and may-
hem and the courageous or lucky surviving to another day.
Can a legend not just stay dead?*

A night and a day of relentless fighting meant that Koorland no longer heard the thump of exploding shells and
the crackle of bolters and lasguns. He was as deaf to it as
the roars and groans of the orks and the growing prickle at
the nape of his neck that increased with proximity to the
brute-shield.

He vaulted over the broken remains of a courtyard wall,
landing messily in the bolt-ruined corpses of the orks that
had been defending the barrier a minute earlier. Thane and
his Fists Exemplar moved through the rubble to either side.
Lascannon and autocannon fire flared and shrieked overhead from the Land Raiders and Predators pushing up
behind the Space Marines' thrust. Further out, companies
from the rest of the multi-Chapter taskforce speared into

the desolation unleashed by the big guns of the Astra Militarum and the bombs of the Navy.

The setting sun carved stark shadows from the jutting remnants of walls and stairwells, the heaps of collapsed roofs, making dark pits of exposed cellars and sub-levels.

A distinct crack sounded through the din of other battle noise, sharper than thunder, longer than the report of a cannon. An instant later a bolt of red flew past the advancing Space Marines, striking a Crimson Fists Predator. The blast passed through the turret armour, leaving a neat hole. Its exit through the engine block was far more explosive, turning fuel and batteries into an incendiary blast that shot out ten metres, scattering flaming shrapnel.

In seconds the other vehicles returned fire, tracing the trajectory of the attack to an armoured bunker that squatted over the ruins on an outcrop of bomb-cratered rock. Lascannon beams and shells ricocheted harmlessly from a gleaming wall of energy that sprang into life around it.

The squads pushed on, concentrating their bolter fire on the orks still holding the ruins ahead. Corkscrewing rockets and rapid-fire bullets whined out of the dust clouds in reply.

The ork gun fired again, this time slashing through the frontal armour of a Vindicator tank that had been crawling forward, its demolisher cannon intending to breach the gates of the fortifications guarding the gun tower. The muzzle flare of smaller weapons sparkled along revetments and from firing slits, the fusillade lashing down at the brightly-armoured warriors pushing through the smoke and rubble.

'We cannot afford to lose more armour!' Quesadra's vox-carried assessment was as accurate as it was brief.

'Air support?' suggested Thane. 'Knights?'

'Anti-air batteries still active,' replied Koorland. 'The Knight battalions are supporting the western flank. Analysis has revealed a weakness in the orks' chronobiology. They seem to be more sluggish around twilight. We need to be at the shield-line by dusk. We'll have to do this ourselves.'

A shadow swallowed Koorland as Vulkan caught up with him. The primarch paid no attention to the weapons fire exploding all around them, turning his helmeted head left and right as he surveyed the scene.

'Armoured gate, Lord Commander,' Vulkan told Koorland. Bullets skipped from his plastron and shoulder pauldrons as he raised to point a little to the right.

Koorland looked, magnifying his suit's auto-senses. Through the swirl of grime and smoke he could see the portal, hidden between two craggy outcrops surrounded by mounds of broken masonry and tangled metal.

The ork emplacement fired again, turning a second Predator to slag and broken armour plates.

'We must pull the armour back, brother-commander,' said Thane, coming up from behind Koorland, two squads of Fists Exemplar with him.

'Vehicle support, withdraw five hundred metres,' Koorland announced over the vox. 'Devastator squads attend for new orders.'

Bohemond arrived out of the battle fog moments later, leading nearly two hundred black-armoured Space Marines – his personal guard bolstered by warriors drawn from other companies. He did not pause but broke out of the ruined buildings across the square beyond, into the teeth of the ork defensive fire. Several of his Space Marines fell to a converging storm of heavy weapons fire, yet the High Marshal's warriors gained ground quickly and took up firing positions from which they could target the orks ringing the hill-bunker.

'Advance!' called Koorland, taking advantage of the Black Templars assault. The Lord Commander surged across the shifting piles of rubble, Vulkan striding alongside. Koorland's sprint finished in the cover of a broken archway just a hundred metres from the fortification's gatehouse.

The force shield sparked and flared as Devastators levelled their heavy bolters and lascannons at the portal. Secondary turrets mounted on the pinnacles of rock flanking the gate opened fire, pulverising rubble and armour with rapid bursts of blue plasma. Dragging their dead and wounded companions with them, several Space Marine squads were forced back into the ruins.

'We cannot just stay here,' snarled Bohemond. 'Koorland, give the order to attack!'

Koorland hesitated, trying to find another way of opening up the fortress.

'What manner of Lord Commander are you?' Bohemond continued. 'Lord Vulkan, I have held my tongue, but now I must speak. Our brother of the Imperial Fists would barely make the rank of Chapter Master in better times. Why do you support him as Lord Commander?'

The primarch said nothing.

'We're still outside their field,' remarked Thane. 'How do we breach the gate?'

'With this,' said Vulkan, brandishing Doomtremor. He

looked at Bohemond and tossed the weapon onto a pile of rubble a few metres ahead of their position. 'High Marshal, prove to me you are worthy of my support instead of Koorland.'

Bohemond did not hesitate, but burst from the ruins. A single blast from his jump pack took him to the massive hammer. Seizing the haft in both hands, he tried to lift Doomtremor. It barely rose a few centimetres, servos whining in the Black Templar's armour. A second later he dropped the hammer and staggered away.

'Any others?' Vulkan announced. He pointed at Quesadra. 'Crimson Fist, would you be Lord Commander instead?'

'If you will it, lord primarch,' replied the Chapter Master.

Bullets pinged from the rubble as he advanced. Bohemond stepped back with a shake of the head.

'It is a trick, brother, nothing more.' The Black Templar stalked back to his warriors while Quesadra strained to lift the primarch's hammer without success.

Koorland watched all of this in silence, wondering what Vulkan was trying to prove.

'Lord Commander, your turn,' said the towering warrior, waving a hand towards Doomtremor.

'You wish me to use your hammer to break the gate of the fortress, Lord Vulkan?' said Koorland, holstering his pistol. 'Is that the challenge?'

'It is.'

Koorland looked at Doomtremor and then the gate and back to the power hammer. It was clear none but Vulkan had the strength to lift it conventionally. The Lord Commander raised a hand to the Fists Exemplar beside him.

'Thane, bring your squad with me.'

Koorland set off over the rubble, the Fists Exemplar in tow. At his direction, Thane and two others helped him take up Doomtremor, like a siege ram of ancient times.

'Cover fire!' ordered Koorland, breaking into a run, the others matching his pace. The remaining Fists Exemplar poured what fire they could towards the slits and ramparts of the gate-crags.

Bullets spitting past them, explosions tearing up dirt and brick in their wake, Koorland's assault team dashed between the crag-towers, lifting Doomtremor to their shoulders. Bolt impacts and lascannon blasts spattered them with splinters and molten rock from the walls above.

'Now!' Koorland told his companions. They hurled Doomtremor as a javelin. Head wreathed in lightning, the hammer struck the gate like a thunderbolt. Metal shattered under the impact, the detonation of power shearing the entire gate from its mounting.

The Lord Commander and his warriors drew their weapons to open fire at the stunned orks within, stepping into a mist of molten steel. Koorland felt the tread of Vulkan approaching a second before the primarch passed, snatching up Doomtremor to wade into the greenskins with broad sweeps of the gleaming hammer.

'There is more to the rank of Lord Commander than being the best fighter, Bohemond,' the primarch called out, voice stern. 'Great warriors follow the greatest leader.'

CHAPTER ELEVEN

Ullanor – Gorkogrod

The anarchic sprawl of the outer city butted up against larger, more purpose-built edifices in central Gorkogrod. The maze of overlapping roofs and walkways, the cable runs and subterranean tunnels, winding alleys and semi-derelict construction sites that had enabled the Assassin to move this close abruptly stopped.

Heading into Gorkogrod, Esad Wire found evidence of the workforce that had built the city: human corpses, left out where vermin and smaller greenskins picked at flesh and bones. Not only humans had given their lives in the labour – a few eldar and species he could not identify shared the mass graves with the Emperor's servants. He came across filthy, half-collapsed cage-houses and cell blocks that must have held thousands of slaves in this quarter alone. The orks' smaller cousins, the gretchin, had claimed these prisons in the shadow of the great fortresses of their overlords, and turned them into shanties that were home to hundreds of screeching, bickering aliens.

He ditched the buggy about four kilometres from where he had taken it. Contrary to their previous apathy, the orks had mustered from their barracks and shanty-houses when starships started falling from the skies. On foot his progress was slower but more assured, but now he faced a fresh challenge.

Beast Krule had hoped that the fall of night would assist him, but the roads of the inner city were lit with bright lamps while searchlights cut the sky to aid the anti-aircraft guns that jutted from the roofs like the thorns of a bush. The orks were out in numbers, hundreds trudging down into the ghetto, as many riding on battlewagons, trikes, buggies and other vehicles. He had seen nothing of the larger war engines, but he knew that they had to be somewhere, possibly using a more accessible route out of the city.

Crouched in the shadow of a chimney stack, Krule watched the near-endless procession of aliens going past. It seemed to him as much a carnival as a war mustering, reminding him of the ranting, self-flagellating zealots that sometimes gathered outside the great shrines that had been erected in worship of the Emperor. There were banners and icons depicting orkish faces, surrounded by glyph-runes he could not decipher, which he assumed might be devotions and prayers.

Quite a lot of the orks seemed to be drunk – at least as far as Krule could tell with his limited experience. They had barrels and bottles that they repeatedly drank from, slopping thick liquid into large cups and raising them in toast to each other. Gretchin scurried everywhere, fetching and carrying weapons, ammunition, roasted meat on skewers, shiny baubles and everything else beside. They clung to the footplates and roll bars of the wagons, and scampered underfoot through the crowds of marching orks, some of them clearly selling wares, others simply trying not to be trodden underfoot.

Krule jumped to the next roof. He had cast off his ork-ish disguise in favour of a return to cameleoline stealth and unhindered agility. From this new vantage point the Assassin could see further up the broad street, to a pair of reinforced towers flanking the highway. There didn't seem to be actual gates, but the road was barred by a body of ork warriors in what appeared to be uniforms – nothing quite so elaborate as the dress style of the Astra Militarum, but the two dozen or so xenos wore black flak jackets reinforced with rivets, and square back banners emblazoned with sig-ils of a red fist.

These guards patrolled back and forth, clubbing lesser warriors seemingly at random, sometimes stopping a truck or buggy to extract information or possibly bribes from those aboard.

If there was one blessing to be found in the mobilisation, it was that Krule knew he would not be heard. The orks' laughter and shouts competed with the snarl of engines. On the open beds of some of the transports orks drummed with more enthusiasm than rhythm, and thrashed at amplified string instruments, chanting and bellowing along to their battle-music. Others listened to portable vox-casters, a hor-rendous cacophony blaring from speakers attached to their vehicles or carried by diminutive assistants.

Krule's eye was drawn to a peculiar couple of orks a little

distance from the gate. The two of them stood on crates and shouted at the passing greenskins from their vantage point. A crowd of gretchin holding placards filled with ork glyphs surrounded them. Sometimes one of the orks would reach into a sack and scatter handfuls of shells and bullets into the crowd while the other bared its fangs, raised its hands in the air and shook its fists even more vigorously. Many of the greenskins stopped to pick up the thrown ammunition, clasping the bullets in their fists and bellowing approval to the two orks. More gretchin tumbled and fought through the legs of their betters trying to get as many of the gift-shells as possible, snapping and clawing. The Assassin watched this behaviour for several minutes until he realised what the cajoling, bullet-scattering orks were doing.

They were preaching.

While the great minds of the Imperium had been focused on anticipating what new machines and warriors might emerge from this accelerated development of the orks, none had considered the emergence of other social constructs such as music and entertainment. And just as the Ecclesiarchy had risen in power in recent centuries, so it seemed that religion was also emerging in the ranks of the orks.

Beast continued towards the divide between shanty and city proper. He moved away from the main thoroughfare to where it was darker. Beneath the shadow of the great fortress-buildings ringing the upper mountain, the narrower roads were choked with rocks, metal, rubble and trash – detritus thrown down from roofs and storeys above or simply left heaped where it had been discarded during construction of the inner city.

The compounds and shanty-terraces were abandoned but Krule was pleased to see that the buildings were still mostly intact and butted directly up to the outer walls of the higher citadels. The foundations were made from a type of ferrocrete, soft enough for his reinforced fingers to make handholds.

A spidery darker shadow in the night, Beast Krule climbed.

It took several minutes, moving past lit windows and iron-railed walkways, until he reached a rampart isolated from any view of the upper fortifications. He pulled himself over the ledge and onto the walkway.

A door swung open to his right, spilling blue light onto the rampart. Krule's cameleoline shifted rapidly, trying to adjust from total darkness to the grey of artificial stone. Something grunted in the doorway, stepping out.

Krule sprang, lancing his mono-stiletto through the ork's left eye, piercing the brain. He rode the body down as it crashed to the hard floor. He looked up, finding himself at the threshold of some kind of guard room or barracks dorm. Three orks sat around a table tossing glyph-marked tiles, moving small metal effigies across a triangular board. Steaming mugs sat beside their game, along with bowls that held chewed bones and remnants of other food.

The orks looked up at the commotion, red eyes widening in shock.

Combat stimms flooded his body. Krule threw himself into the room, his needler coughing projectiles into the face of the ork furthest from the door. The alien warrior slumped, twitching as anti-xenos toxins shut down its organs. The closest ork rose from a sagging couch, tugging madly at the pistol in its belt. The Assassin's fist found its gaping mouth, shattering its jaw and crushing its throat with a spray of thick blood.

The third pushed itself towards another door, or rather the vox-set visible in the room beyond, shouting a warning. Krule felled it with more needler fire and burst into the adjacent chamber.

Two gretchin manned the communications system. They spun on their stools. Krule snapped the arm of the one reaching towards a vox-pickup and kicked the other into the wall. Half a second later his fists cut short their horrified squeaks and hisses.

Crouched in the doorway, he waited and listened.

A minute passed. Nothing came.

Krule stalked back to the exterior and glanced down to the outer city. The lamps and lanterns of the orks made rivers of fire pouring towards the distant plains. Looking further still he could see the small stars of aircraft jets and the red blossoms of artillery detonations. The view crackled and sparked where shells and missiles hit the force field protecting the city. Many would die in the assault, thousands or tens of thousands, but it was unavoidable. The greater the fury thrown at the city, the more opportunity for Krule to get to his target and strike.

The best way to help mankind in the grander scheme, and those battling for Gorkogrod, was to kill the Great Beast.

Invigorated by these thoughts, Krule started to climb again, seeking a vantage point from which he would be able to plan the next phase of the infiltration.

CHAPTER TWELVE

Ullanor – Gorkogrod

As he ripped free his sword from the ork's gut, blood sprayed across Bohemond. His tabard was already soaked in the gore of his foes, clinging to the black enamelled plates of his armour. He stepped to the right, letting the body slump atop the other corpses piled around him, bringing up the long blade to stop the swing of a power-wreathed claw.

'We are but vessels for a divine wrath!' the High Marshal bellowed to his warriors. 'Into us is poured the ire of the Emperor and in our veins it boils. Your blade is His blade, your blood is His blood.'

Bohemond stepped inside the reach of the ork and slammed the brow of his helm into its jaw, snapping teeth and bone. The alien's snarl turned to a howl of pain. Bohemond ducked its clumsy swipe and hacked his sword into the exposed midriff, his blue-gleaming blade slicing easily through layers of studded metal plating. Drawing the sword out, he spun and chopped, severing the creature's arm.

Beside him, Clermont was firing his bolter into the ruins

on the far side of a collapsed bridge, the rest of the castellan's squad providing more cover fire. The river that gurgled below was so choked with filth, bodies and debris that it was impossible to tell if it had ever been fresh or was just an exposed sewer. It steamed in the heat of the midday sun.

Just ahead of Bohemond a shell detonated against the remains of the bridge's arch, showering him with fist-sized chunks of rubble. Stonework swayed and then collapsed, tumbling down the short ravine to dam the river even more.

'Incoming vehicles,' warned Brother Derneicht. 'Multiple sig–'

The auspex-bearer was cut off by a massive tracked battle-wagon rearing up over the mounds of rubble beside him, a huge spiked roller turning on arms mounted at its front. The machine slammed down into the rubble, crushing Derneicht and another Black Templar beneath the roller. Pieces of flesh and shattered ceramite flew in all directions as the behemoth churned towards the other squads. It was easily as large as a Land Raider, two turrets flanking a high-sided driver's cab, their heavy weapons spitting rounds into the Space Marines.

Their engines a higher-pitched scream, three warbikes hurtled over the crest behind the battlefortress, wide-slung chainguns spewing haphazard salvoes. A fourth sped into view, jumping over the ridge. A shot from Clermont took off half the rider's head and the warbike crashed flaming into the mess of broken masonry.

'With me! Let not the size of the foe weight your thoughts,' Bohemond roared, sprinting towards the battlefortress. From a slatted troop compartment behind the turrets, more orks threw stick-bombs at the onrushing Black Templars. Explosions and metal fragments engulfed them, but Bohemond pressed on through the smoke and dust.

He slightly misjudged the position of the battlefortress. It loomed out of the smoke, accelerating hard, just a few metres away. Jump pack flaring, Bohemond leapt, clearing the deadly cylinder. Behind him Brother Cadrallus was not so fortunate, and disappeared beneath blood-slicked, rubble-choked spikes.

Bohemond hewed through the retaining cage of the driver's armoured cab, peeling back the roof like the lid of a ration tin. The driver looked up, firing a pistol with its free hand, the other chained to a thick-rimmed steering wheel. Bullets cracked from the High Marshal's faceplate.

The cab was too confined for Bohemond's blade. He punched down with all of the weight and strength of his battleplate, crushing the ork's head with a single blow. An axe skittered across Bohemond's pauldron and he turned, sword licking out instinctively to slash the face of his assailant. The ork fell back with a whine of pain. Other greenskins clambered out of the transport cage, climbing over whirring tracks and spinning turret gears.

With jump packs shrieking more Black Templars arrived, bodily landing on some of the orks, blades and pistols hacking and roaring to cut down others. A particularly well-armoured foe pulled itself out of the turret behind Bohemond and threw itself at him, bearing them both over with its momentum. They rolled twice, metal buckling under their bulk. Bohemond's hand struck a trembling exhaust stack, jarring his blade from his grip. It dangled over churning treads, linked to his wrist by a length of gilded chain, just centimetres from being drawn into the grinding road wheels powering the track.

Pinning the Black Templar's other hand beneath its bulk, the ork smashed the haft of its axe into Bohemond's face, cracking his left eye-lens. It drew its arm back for another blow.

Clermont was there as the axe head reached the apex of its backswing. His armoured boot crashed into the side of the ork, knocking it over. Three rapid rounds from the castellan's bolter obliterated the alien's chest, bolts punching through armour to detonate inside the creature's ribcage.

The battlefortress still careened onwards, the slumped driver's body taking it in a curve towards the rubble-choked waterway. Drawing up his sword, Bohemond stood. He looked down the ridge from the extra height of the engine deck, to where a pall of smoke and dozens of vague silhouettes betrayed the approach of even more vehicles.

He leapt from the mobile fortress, his battle-brothers following. They landed awkwardly in the hillocks of broken stone and shattered corpses. A few seconds later the ork tank disappeared over the lip of the waterway. The crash of its descent masked the increasing growl of engines drawing closer.

Two warbikes still raced around the Space Marines, their autocannons blazing, chased by a storm of bolter flares from the encircled Black Templars. Large humanoid shapes appeared from the murk – more orks, piloting Dreadnought-like walkers with heavy weapons and pincer-clawed arms. One strode past Brother Sigurd, brushing the Space Marine aside with a back-handed blow.

While bolts sparked from its armour the walker swiped at Bohemond, trying to seize hold of his arm. He dodged the clumsy attack and, sword in both hands, set about hacking away the offending limb.

'Signal Dorr,' he barked at Clermont. 'We need that flying column of tanks he promised us. Without air or war machine support inside the shield, we cannot hold.'

The High Marshal rolled aside as the ork walker tried to shred him with a point-blank burst of weapons fire. He cut the cables of its legs, pinning it in place with a spray of dark hydraulic fluids.

'Retreat, High Marshal?' Clermont sounded incredulous. 'What about taking not one step back?'

'Sometimes, castellan...' Bohemond paused while he rammed the full length of his sword between two armoured plates, piercing the walker with a metre and a half of power-field-encased blade. Something shrieked inside the machine and its metal limbs rattled with sympathetic death throes. Bohemond dragged out the sword, blood hissing from its field.

'Sometimes, castellan,' he started again, 'you need to take a step back to get a proper swing.'

Galtan continued to read from the list scrolling across the face of his data-slate, rocked left and right as the *Dorn's Ire* swayed and lurched over hills made of levelled buildings.

'Twenty-three aircraft remaining, including four strategic bombers. Tech-priests are working as fast as possible to bring the *Scornful* back to battle-readiness. We really could do with that Stormblade at the moment.'

'That's enough of what we have, or rather don't have. What about the enemy?' said Dorr. He swung his chair towards the plate of the cartolith, its surface flickering with tiny holograms of runes depicting the latest dispositional data.

The gunners in the secondary sponsons opened fire. On external pict-feed displays Dorr saw that they were raking the burning wreckage of several ork heavy transports, ensuring nothing had survived the battlecannon blasts that had destroyed them a few minutes earlier. Galtan waited patiently for the din of their fire to stop.

'Super-heavy tanks and walkers... nothing Titan-class as yet, field-legatus,' he replied between bursts of dual heavy bolters. 'A surprising lack of air power, but more than compensated for by a plethora of anti-aircraft rocket batteries and self-propelled guns.'

'And the brute-shield,' one of the subalterns added with a grimace.

'Yes, best not to forget that,' said Dorr. He returned his attention to Galtan. 'What about infantry?'

'In all honesty, we're outclassed, field-legatus. We lost half our companies in the orbital strike. Starting from such a poor base, we could never match the orks' numbers. Without the Space Marines we would never have reached this far.'

Dorr absorbed this brutal assessment in silence, rubbing his whiskered chin. His valet and personal kit had been lost with the *Praetor Fidelis*, along with a company of his best storm troopers and the majority of his logistical and strategos teams.

'On the other hand,' Galtan added with forced cheerfulness, 'if it wasn't for us, the Space Marines would have been overrun within hours.'

'We're stretched too thin,' the field-legatus remarked, waving a hand towards the strategic display. 'This was supposed to be a concentrated thrust into the city. The ork attacks have dragged us out to the flanks, pulling us away from the Space Marines.'

'A quirk of the city's layout, field-legatus,' said Galtan.

'Yes, I know that!' snapped the field-legatus, banging a fist on the console panel. He drew in a breath, shaking his head. 'This city is not as ramshackle and anarchic as it looks, is it? Kill-channels, underground supply routes, layered defences. A well-planned structure hiding under hovels and scrapyards!'

'We believe we have engaged a significant part of the ork forces, field-legatus,' said another subaltern – one with curly hair and bright blue eyes, called Festria or Fenestris or something like that. 'Far more than we should have been able to, considering our deplorable state at the outset. The Adeptus Mechanicus have been making far swifter progress.'

'Yes, Zhokuv's latest communiqué suggested as much,' said Dorr. He leaned his chair back, crossing his arms. 'Perhaps they could have spared us a Knight or two, maybe even a Titan.' He sighed. 'There's nothing more to be done, except press on where we can and hold ground where we cannot.'

And hope the warlords of Mars can bring down the field before we are destroyed, he added to himself.

CHAPTER THIRTEEN

Ullanor – outer Gorkogrod

Sometimes the dream returns. A fantasy. A phantasm. Just one more year. One more year before Davin. What might have been? What might we have accomplished? Another year before Ullanor, perhaps. Another year in the presence of the Emperor, another step closer to the victory He had seen.

But it was false, even then. Do not tell me about falsehood. It lies in the hearts of all men and women, waiting to be nurtured by vanity and lies.

But if mankind were not weak and broken, that would be even more dreadful.

Though the reach of the magos dominus' mightiest engines stopped at the brute-shield, they were not without impact. The nobles of the Knight Houses had long sworn fealty to Mars, and on the battlefields of Ullanor they adhered to those ancient oaths through the fiercest fighting.

A dozen metres tall, the ancient walkers of the Knight Scions stalked the ruins of Gorkogrod seeking the enemy wherever they could be found. Unhindered by the broken terrain, the massive Knight suits pushed forward where tanks could not, carving into the enemy and laying waste to the city itself.

Knights Paladin led the line, their battle cannons breaking ork mobs as easily as they crumpled the armour of tanks and transports. Chainswords several metres long were more than a match for the claws and buzzsaws of ork heavy dreadnoughts and mega-armoured nobles. With the Paladins came Knights Errant with thermal cannons to vaporise metal and flesh, the flanks of their squadrons secured by darting forays by paired Knights Lancer.

Directional ion fields crackling under incessant barrages from ork artillery and tank guns, the towering Knights Castellan and Crusader were bastions around which the infantry of the Adeptus Mechanicus could hinge their attacks. Battle servitors and carapace-suited skitarii flooded the ruins, a wall of red every bit as relentless as the ork waves that crashed against them.

The Great Beast showed its cunning here also, harbouring its forces well, committing them only when needed. Where the Knights strode, infantry and light vehicles attempted to speed past to strike into the rear of the advancing Cult Mechanicus. Where the Knights were not, the weight of battlefortresses and super-heavy stompers – war engines a match for any Imperial Knight in bulk and firepower – was pressed hardest. But no amount of raw strategy could guard against the meticulous encroachment of the Martian warriors, guided by machine intelligences and the most sophisticated battle-augurs.

Zhokuv wielded the men, servitors, tanks, automata and war engines like an overseer of a manufactory, driving them on hard but weighing every loss against potential gains, seeking efficiencies with ruthless precision. Like the gears of a machine the Martian army continued to grind on. Sometimes the Mechanicus overpowered the orks through sheer force of guns, machines and men. At other times they used superior logistics to draw the greenskins into ambushes or outpace them with rapid flank attacks that cut them off from their support coming from the inner city.

Block by block, street by street, the Adeptus Mechanicus took Gorkogrod, until the lead echelons of Kataphron cyborgs and Praetorian heavy servitors were a kilometre inside the brute-shield. Thousands of Martian veterans swarmed forward to occupy abandoned bunkers, while tech-priests and magi seized and analysed what they could of the ork technology in the hopes of discerning some secret of how the brute-shield worked or was powered.

Much to the dismay of his less bellicose advisors, Zhokuv left the command headquarters protected by the Warlord Titans and sought to view the new front line in person. Escorted by Knights Warden and Knights Castigator of House Taranis, the dominus sallied forth in his battle shell.

Riding behind in a tracked armoured car, Laurentis and others of the inner cadre looked in awe at the devastation that had been brought to Gorkogrod. Of the city they had seen on the initial scans and vid-streams, only the inner reaches remained. The mountainside was littered with ruins and the remnants of war engines both human and ork. Shell craters were criss-crossed by seared trenches from volcano cannons, marked by glassy bowls of plasma detonations.

They were no more than fifteen hundred metres from the brute-shield, which could be clearly seen as a shimmering curtain cutting across the rubble-strewn ridge ahead. Picking up urgent broad-channel transmissions from the vanguard companies, Zhokuv ordered his retinue to stop.

'What is it, dominus?' asked Sir Valek, piloting the Knight Warden *Red Warrior*. He brought his machine to a halt astride the broken highway, its gatling cannon and missile launcher poised to deliver a blistering fusillade at anything approaching from the city centre.

'Ork counter-attack, rapid advance against our positions,' Zhokuv informed his companions, broadcasting to the magi and pilots. To the Knight Scions, he added, 'Move forward and engage.'

'We are tasked with your protection, dominus,' Sir Valek protested.

Zhokuv voxed back, sending a chastisement code into the system of Valek's Knight that marked the machine and pilot for censure at a future date. 'The surest way to guarantee our safety is a swift end to this mounting assault.'

The Knight pilots confirmed their orders and strode ahead, weapons at the ready. Zhokuv patched his visual feeds into the data-receptors of the *Red Warrior*, as he had done with the scout-craft at the start of the planetary assault. He felt the limbs of the ancient war machine bunching and flexing as if they were his own, glorying in the sensation of power emanating from his reactor. Valek's presence was like a fly on his back, barely noticed in the midst of the war machine.

Ahead, flurries of explosions lit the landscape – detonations unlike anything they had seen since landing. Coruscations of green energy flowed upwards like flames in slow motion, carrying with them avalanches of debris. It took a moment for Zhokuv to adjust to the perspective of the Knight. As he did so, calculating the range to the closest detonation, he realised that some of the lumps of debris were Kataphrons and battle tanks, tossed into the air like the toys of a petulant child.

Shapes larger than Knights bulled their way through the buildings, brushing them aside with their bulk. Small arms and heavy weapons were equally ineffective against their power fields, sparks of red against the immensity of the new war engines. Anti-tank cannons strobed las and tracers into the ruins, shredding stone and soldier with equal ease. Massive belly guns belched fire and sent tank-sized shells crashing into the waves of red-armoured skitarii falling back from the assault.

The Great Beast had finally despatched its gargants.

Zhokuv immediately transmitted a withdrawal order to the beset infantry phalanx, channelling the command via the *Red Warrior* to boost its reach. Needing no further encouragement, robed tech-priests, clanking cybernetica constructs and Martian soldiers broke cover and flowed back down the city-mountain in droves, but the gargants paid them little heed. They continued on, emerging from the brute-shield to take on the assembled Knight squadrons.

The fire of the macro-cannons and gatling blasters of the Knights lit the lead gargant from base to head, power fields flickering with scarlet lightning. The ork war machines returned fire, bolts of energy and ripples of shells slamming into the gleaming ion shields of the Martian walkers. Wayward las-beams and cannon strikes ripped swathes through the few buildings still standing, turning multi-storey fortifications and half-broken towers into falling rubble and billowing dust clouds.

Yet for all he strained the sensory array of the Knight Warden and scanned back and forth across the data-streams, Zhokuv could find nothing that explained the extraordinary detonations and anarchy that had heralded the counter-attack. The *Red Warrior* advanced another hundred metres, its guns targeting the failing energy defences of the closest gargant. The dominus spied smaller war engines rumbling and striding through the clouds of exhaust and dust that swathed the gargants.

Some were tracked or wheeled battletowers, arcs of green lightning forking from their summits. With them came more gargants, amongst their rockets and guns crane-like appendages that fired crackling emerald stars. Fronds of wreathing jade flame wrapped around Kataphrons and skitarii, dragging them into whirling maelstroms of devastating energy.

Advancing past the gargants which duelled with newly-arrived Titans, the battletowers turned their otherworldly powers upon the Knights. Against physical attacks their ion shields provided some protection, but many were struck by phantamagorical bolts that passed straight through such defences, turning armour inside out, as though invisible hands ripped them asunder from within.

Flurries of psychic energy pummelled the plates of a

Knight, crushing it into the ground with repeated blows that buckled armour and bent internal struts like grass. Waves of fire rippled out from a trio of battlewagons connected to each other by sparking cables. The inferno of psychic energy licked up the legs and body of a Knight Castigator, causing the ammunition of its bolt cannon to explode in the hopper. Zhokuv felt the loss of connection with the pilot as he was burned alive inside the cockpit.

Together the gargants and psychic engines advanced again. In their wake came a flood of maddened orks, frothing and spitting, each as large as a common ork chieftain. Huge detonations of psychic power wracked the Cult Mechanicus lines, leaving blasted craters in their wake looking oddly like trails of monstrous footsteps.

Faced with such a combination of brute power and insidious attack there was nothing Knights or skitarii, tech-priests or Kataphrons could do except pull back.

Rune Priest Thorild sensed waves of anger emanating from the primarch. Fully armoured, expression concealed within his dragonet helm, his body language spoke of repose, but the emotions leaking through the iron will of Vulkan said otherwise.

On hearing the news of the Adeptus Mechanicus setback, the gene-father of the Salamanders had demanded a Thunderhawk and as many Librarians as could be quickly mustered. The Lord Commander had argued that if the Space Marines could penetrate deeper into the inner city on another front, the Great Beast would be forced to pull back its greatest war engines and psykers to combat the threat. But such logic only triggered a rare outburst, a direct order from the primarch, evidence of Vulkan's barely contained wrath.

Cowed, Koorland had assembled from the Chapters to hand the small company that rode with the primarch towards the heart of the ork offensive. Other Space Marine forces followed to provide a more physical back-up to the Librarians' otherworldly powers. Bohemond had not outright refused to join the mission, but had made it clear he wanted no part of it, claiming the need for his presence elsewhere was greater.

The Space Wolf also felt the presence of the others – Gandorin and Adarian most strongly, but also lesser-ranked psykers of several Chapters. The remaining survivors of the first connection with the orks had been charged to watch the other psychic assets of the force, to ensure no further contamination from the raging psychic power of the orks.

'Pardon my asking, Lord Vulkan, but I cannot help but sense you are taking this personally,' said Epistolary Kalvis of the Crimson Fists. 'Given experience in earlier interaction with the background ork psychic presence, is this wise?'

Vulkan did not turn his head.

'We must fight fire with fire,' he said quietly.

None of the other Librarians spoke, but Kalvis persisted, perhaps feeling it was his duty to speak out, or simply holding a personal unease at their immediate future.

'What exactly do you intend, Lord Vulkan? It pains me to say, but we cannot match the psychic might of the orks.'

'You just have to contain them long enough for me to kill them,' growled the primarch. He straightened and looked at the assembled psykers. 'During the Great Crusade we met many strange creatures and warp-born horrors. We knew little of psychic power and its true source, for the Emperor had chosen ignorance to be our shield against temptation. But we knew enough. That some foes cannot be beaten by bullets and blades, but with the power of the mind. In His wisdom He did not tell us of daemons and gods, of course.'

Thorild shifted nervously. He knew of what the primarch spoke. The others were similarly uncomfortable, sharing the belief that such matters, such entities were not for casual conversation. Vulkan seemed oblivious to their unease, or uncaring of it, and continued.

'But the Emperor had a secret army to combat the threat of the psychic and the daemonic. His Sisters of Silence, we called them. Anti-psykers trained as warrior-maidens. One in trillions, each of them, but across the great vastness of humanity they were number enough. What I would give for a company of the Silent Sisterhood now...'

'I do not think the Sisters of Silence have survived, lord primarch,' said Gandorin.

'We will do what we can,' said Thorild, 'but we risk further ruin if we dare too much, lord primarch. To treat too long with the powers of the Great Beast is to open ours–'

'Do not speak to me of temptation and powers, rune-wielder,' Vulkan said heavily. The eyes of his helm seemed to take on a different gleam, but it had to be a trick of the Thunderhawk's lighting. 'When you have looked upon the face of your brothers and seen strangers, when you have seen the entire galaxy burn for the whims of Dark Gods...

Or stood for an eternity at the breach to keep the ravening powers from destroying all that you love...'

'We have incoming counter-air fire, Lord Vulkan,' announced the pilot. 'Where do you want to set down?'

'Get as close as you can,' the primarch replied. He stood up and moved to the front assault ramp, head bent beneath the ceiling of the troop deck. 'There will be no need to land.'

The muffled thump of flak shells and the rattle of shrapnel on the hull mixed with the growl of the engines. The pilot moved the gunship in tight turns to evade the worst of the incoming fire but Thorild felt the anxiety of his brothers even above the mounting anticipation of the primarch.

'Do all that you can to suppress their powers, that is all I ask,' Vulkan told them. 'Keep close, shield me with your thoughts.'

He opened the main ramp, air screaming into the troop compartment. Thorild could see the ruined city whipping past a hundred metres below. Titans and Knights duelled with gargants and stompers, heavy weapons pounding out destruction, tank-sized fists and blades that could demolish buildings smashing and slamming against each other. Skitarii and greenskins ripped into each other in firefights and desperate melee across broken buildings. Flickering psychic fires spewed and monstrous apparitions thrashed above the ork horde on the edge of vision.

Almost directly below them waddled a great gargant, thirty metres tall, its huge rotund hull jutting with pylons and copper coils that crackled with green sparks. Upon its shoulders several ork psykers were chained, absorbing the latent savagery of the greenskins around them. Thorild could feel the power churning around the machine. Even as he detected the release of psychic energy a flare of green lightning spat from the psykers, lancing into a column of battle tanks that tried to hold back the ork offensive.

Thorild could feel the wider ork psychic presence like a living thing, seething at the attack on its city, bloating and growing with rage at the human invasion.

'The harder we attack, the stronger the ork psychic effect becomes,' said Adarian, sensing it also.

Thorild nodded. He moved up beside Vulkan.

'You knew the Wolf well, my lord?' he asked.

'We were friends as well as brothers,' Vulkan replied.

'And you trusted him, Lord Vulkan?'

'Several times with my life and the lives of my sons.'

'Then trust me, son of the Wolf. We will not fail you.'

The primarch looked at him and nodded. A second later, he threw himself from the assault ramp.

Thorild watched Vulkan fall, Doomtremor trailing sparks like a comet. The primarch had timed his jump to perfection, hitting the upper deck of the gargant, the impact sending him crashing through the tower and through the armoured plates into the depths below.

A roar of instinctual protest swelled up from the orks' psychic manifestation, but in the depths of the gargant the primal shout was quickly silenced.

'Now, brothers,' Thorild commanded, opening his thoughts to the other Librarians. 'Let us show this savage, and the primarch, what the Adeptus Astartes are truly capable of.'

Thorild launched his spirit into the roiling green mass

of the ork aura, the minds of his companions on his heels appearing in his thoughts as a snarling wolf pack. He sensed rather than saw Vulkan bursting out of the collapsing gargant, already sprinting towards a battletower just behind it.

Gleaming psychic fangs shredded the green claws coalescing around the primarch. The wolves of the Emperor howled their challenge to the Great Beast.

CHAPTER FOURTEEN

Ullanor – Gorkogrod

And at the end we must face the fact that immortality is a greater burden than mortality. The long death, a slow diminishing of meaning. Why curse us with the knowledge, with the fate that we would outlive all that we built? Did He think to outfox entropy itself?

Was it a pain that He had to share? Companions for eternity, empty totems raised up in memory of those lost in the mists of five hundred lifetimes.

And now I am the one that stands alone and I can take no more of it. There is no healing the wounds of the soul.

Stealth had to be sacrificed for speed on occasion. Gore-drenched, Beast Krule's cameleoline had been of little effectiveness for the past hour anyway. With this thought, he dropped out of the duct he had been using, landing in a clean, whitewashed corridor. Oddly clean, for orks, he thought. Chanting echoed from both directions, slow but forceful.

The ork palace-complex – factory, cathedral and fortress combined – was vast but he could hear the muted rumble of detonations, which told him that the other Imperial forces were getting ever closer.

Even if he could not strike down the Great Beast before they arrived at the gates to the citadel, the Assassin's presence would cause confusion and indecision, which would aid the Adeptus Astartes and their allies in their final onslaught.

A pair of orks turned a corner ahead and he opened fire with the alien weapon he had salvaged from his last victim, gunning them down in a flare of rapid energy blasts. Moving past their smouldering corpses, he turned towards the echoing roar of ork voices. Another greenskin emerged from a doorway right in front of him, gnawing at a bone with its chisel fangs. It barely had time to grunt its surprise before his stiletto pierced its chest.

The ork lashed out, Krule's blade still wedged into its ribs. Its fists cracked against the side of the Assassin's head, dazing him. Cursing the resilience of all greenskins, Beast Krule pulled himself free of the hands grasping for his throat and retaliated with a hammerblow punch of his own, caving in the top of its skull and brain.

Stepping over the corpse, Krule noticed in detached fashion that the food still gripped in its fist looked like a small green-skinned arm, a couple of fingers attached with bloody sinew at one end.

The corridor took him to a large balcony overlooking a hangar-like space. Half a dozen orks leaned on a metal rail as they looked into the depths. At one end of the vast hall was a large statue made of overlapping metal plates, heavily riveted, in the form of a giant squatting ork. It was covered head-to-foot in heavy armour, its fists clad in clawed gloves the size of battle tanks. The walls were stone, made of large blocks each carved with an ork glyph – the story of the rise of the Great Beast, perhaps.

There were more galleries above, below and opposite, lined with bellowing orks. The aliens were all as large as nobles or bigger, many of a size to match the archive descriptions of army warlords. They were heavily armed and armoured, bearing the blazon of the red fist he had seen on banners and walls across the palace.

And below were thousands more, perhaps tens of thousands, a sea of gigantic alien beasts. They chanted and grunted in unison, waving their weapons, whipped into a zealous frenzy by some unseen orator at one end of the massive space. The huge cathedral shook with stamping feet and the girder-vaulted ceiling rang with a deafening shout of praise.

Krule staggered back until his spine touched the cold stone of the wall. Through the fog of stimulants the raging orks were a sea of brutal monsters, their chants distant but deafening.

He had expected an elite guard, but the creatures that thronged the hall were terrifying, far beyond the plans of Vangorich. To the orks, might made right, and the creature that ruled over such a mass of alien nightmares had to be mightier than anything the Imperium had encountered for an age.

With cold dread washing away the vestiges of the

stimm-fugue, Beast Krule realised that his mission was impossible.

Worse still, the entire endeavour could not possibly succeed, not against such a force defending a near-impregnable fortress. The Lord Commander, the lord primarch, tens of thousands of Space Marines and soldiers would die before ever setting foot near the Great Beast.

Thought after thought raced through the Assassin. Years of training and experience crumbled when confronted by the sheer horror of the Great Beast's power. How could the Imperium possibly win against such alien fury incarnate? The war was folly. There was no triumph to be had, only the slim chance of survival.

His breathing became ragged, the tension and fatigue of days crowding into his weary body, all resolve dissipating at the sight of the task ahead.

One of the greenskins just a few metres from Beast Krule sniffed the air heavily and turned its flat head towards him. At the same moment, something large eclipsed the light behind Krule.

Instinct rolled him aside, the crackling fist centimetres from his face prickling his skin with energy discharge. His evasive manoeuvre took him out onto the balcony, closer to the other orks. They turned, glowering and snarling.

The creature that had attacked almost blocked the whole entrance with its bulk. It was dressed in a thick hide coat reinforced with straps of metal and rivets the size of a man's fist. It wore a kilt of the same, and heavy steel-capped boots up to its knees. It swung the power claw again, forcing Beast Krule to duck.

The Assassin fired the stolen ork gun, blasting a fusillade directly into the chest of the alien blocking his escape. Metal and leather turned to smoke and steam, and flesh boiled as the ork stumbled back, staggering to one knee.

With just a split second to act, Beast Krule leapt. Using the knee of the downed ork as a step, he vaulted over the wounded alien. It snatched at his ankle as he passed, but momentum carried him over its shoulder. Landing heavily, he tumbled to his feet and started running.

Action cleared away his dread. A fresh purpose filled him. Anger at himself for his weakness spurred him to renewed effort. Krule's mind still burned with what he had seen in the temple-chamber, and with images of what would happen when that army was unleashed against the unsuspecting Space Marines.

They were so close now, Koorland could almost reach out and touch the immense walls of the central citadel. Progress had been slow, tortuous even, every metre gained inside the brute-shield paid for with death and hardship. And the warriors of the Emperor had paid dearly. Of the Space Marines that had survived to reach the surface of Ullanor, a third had been lost. Amongst the ranks of the Astra Militarum the casualty rate was at nearly fifty per cent. Following the psyker-bolstered offensive of the orks, stopped only by Vulkan's direct intervention, the Adeptus Mechanicus had suffered even more. The host of Mars had been reduced to a handful of Titans and seven fully functional Knights, and these war machines could not pass the brute-shield unmolested.

Countless orks had fallen, their bodies a green carpet under the boots of the Space Marines and the treads of Astra Militarum tanks. Where days before they had clashed over a broken field of rubble, now the Emperor's servants and the Great Beast's savages contested for piles of blood and bones, mounds of shattered vehicles and burning gargant wrecks.

If the next kilometre was anything like the last, there would barely be any Imperial force left to break into the citadel proper.

'Nothing worth fighting for was taken easily,' Vulkan told him, perhaps sensing his mood. 'The orks have bled as much as us. More. Much more.'

'We have been too slow, Lord Vulkan. Too slow.' Koorland smashed a fist into the palm of his other hand. 'They are massing behind us. Three landing sites have been overrun. Two more are surrounded.'

'It was never our intention to leave,' the primarch reminded him. He seemed more than resigned to this fact. Rejuvenated almost. Vulkan had shown more heart for the fight after the disastrous landing than before. The Lord Commander had suspicions about the primarch's motives, but his doubts were vague and of no consequence to the immediate future.

Koorland looked up at the forbidding city-palace and the ring of walls, turrets, towers and gatehouses. Idol-statues topped some of the buildings, of polished gold and chrome. Huge standards the equal in size of any Titan kill-banner flapped along the ramparts. And cannons. Cannons by the hundred.

His gaze slid further upwards, to the oppressive, half-seen crackling dome of the brute-shield. The Lord Commander felt claustrophobic looking at it. He could not shake the idea that, like the rest of Ullanor, its intent was not so much to keep attackers out but to trap them within.

Inside with the Great Beast.

The brute-shield had shrunk a few kilometres, its generators overrun by the Imperial advance. But it still protected the inner city from the ships in orbit, as did the massive guns, missiles and energy cannons within.

'We have to get into the citadel,' Koorland declared. He selected the channel to address the Chapter Masters and other force commanders. 'Prepare for the final assault.'

CHAPTER FIFTEEN

Ullanor – Gorkogrod

We delude ourselves with promises of a better tomorrow. 'If only...' begins the mantra of the weak. We must strive without hope of cessation of effort. We must hold ourselves above ambition, seeking to excel but not to conquer. To build is a fleeting experience, while destruction is eternal. Build not for tomorrow but for today. Fight not for your future, but for the present. The past becomes meaningless in such consideration, but we cannot break free from its shackles.

The universe knows what must happen but panders to whims that wish otherwise. Recognising inevitability is not fatalism. How I loathe this waiting.

As when two pugilists step back by tacit consent to draw a breath before recommencing their fight, a lull descended upon the ork city. While the Lord Commander arrayed his broken companies into new formations and Field-Legatus Dorr drew up his reserves to support the next thrust, the Adeptus Mechanicus scoured the outer city of the remaining pockets of orks to secure the line of attack.

Laurentis had argued, possibly a little too vehemently, that the destruction of the brute-shield was still the paramount objective of the Cult Mechanicus, which was how he found himself tasked with leading an expedition to discover how to do just that. Guarded by maniples of cyber-constructs and several platoons of skitarii, watched over by the Knight Paladin *Greyblade*, he picked through the remains of an ork tower close to the original line of the shield. Taking pict-captures and data readings, he examined the spread of debris and attempted to divine the purpose of several chambers and broken machines within.

'It is an amplifier,' he said aloud. He gestured at Jeddaz, a minor tech-priest who had been assigned to him as attendant for some unknown dereliction of duty. Laurentis pointed to the drops of metal on the walls – conduits for something. 'Here, look. These were a network, melted by whatever blast broke the tower. High-intensity melta residue everywhere, a Knight's thermal cannon I would say. And these rooms, they housed battery cells of some kind.'

'But there are no conduits or projectors,' Jeddaz replied with a sigh. He turned over flattened pots and broken furniture with his mechadendrites, what remained of his face curled in a distasteful sneer as though rifling through effluent.

'Magos, I am detecting an aerial approach on an unexpected vector,' Sir Phaldoron warned from the *Greyblade*.

'An air raid?'

'A single craft, coming out of the inner city.'

'Is it heading towards us?'

'Its course will bring it close. Anti-air batteries in the main force are preparing to engage.'

Laurentis shunted the data-stream from the Knight into his cogitator back-ups, thinking to add the information to the vast repository on the orks he already carried. As he did so, he noticed that the flight path of the aircraft was unlike anything he had recorded from the greenskins.

He tried to quantify what he found. Orks were headlong, instinctual fighters. Their pilots were mostly crazed speed-cultists who valued the thrill of high velocity as much as battle itself. The incoming craft was being... circumspect.

'No!' shouted Laurentis, jamming the *Greyblade*'s communications channel with an override signal. He scrambled out of the bunker and up a pile of gore-strewn ruin, his three mechanical legs making hard work of the incline. He searched the skies and saw the blot that was the incoming aircraft.

'Is it broadcasting any signals? Any identifiers?'

'Why would it...' The Knight Scion trailed off. 'There is a low-frequency radio transmission, magos.'

'Send it to me.'

'It could be-'

'Send it to me! And tell the anti-air to hold fire!'

The Knight Scion obeyed, broadcasting the intercepted transmission into the dataflow of Laurentis. The magos opened up the compact data packet and translated it to audio.

'...must not attack. Overwhelming counter-assault is ready. Is anyone listening to this? I am Esad Wire of the Officio Assassinorum, agent of Lord Vangorich. My mission is sanctioned by Inquisitorial representation. I must speak to the Lord Commander and lord primarch immediately!

Do not attack the citadel! For the love of the Emperor and Mankind, do not attack!'

Surrounded by Chapter Masters, the Assassin was certainly not the most intimidating individual gathered in the bombed-out ruin of an ork storehouse. The presence of Vulkan made his lack of size even more apparent. But Assassins did not rely on physique alone. There was a tension in every movement of Esad Wire, an underlying energy about to be unleashed. Koorland recognised it from his own brothers when preparing for battle – the storm beneath a calm sea.

Esad Wire sat on a broken plinth, his black bodysuit slicked with blood. Most of it was the thick gore of the orks, but some of the Assassin's own leaked through a number of tears in the synskin suit. His shoulders were hunched with fatigue, a finger tapping on one knee with nervous energy.

His eyes were hard as flint, pupils glittering with augment systems. Koorland could also smell a trace of biomechanical oil and artificial sanguinary fluids, indicating internal bionics as well. No surprise, of course, given that all Officio Assassinorum personnel were physically boosted in some fashion. The hidden nature of Wire's augmentations meant that his role was clearly one of disguise and infiltration.

His breath stank of stimm residue and an aura of antiseptic coagulant surrounded the Assassin. As he shifted, a wound opened under his ribs, a fresh trickle of blood dribbling out onto his synskin sheath. The Assassin didn't seem to notice. His attention moved from one Space Marine to

the next and then on again, constantly scouring his surroundings and their occupants.

Esad Wire had crash-landed the ork fighter almost on top
of the Imperial lines, demanding audience with the commanders. Secured by Crimson Fists, he had said nothing
until the representatives of the allied factions had arrived.
The scene for the audience was grim – the broken stone
underfoot was smeared with the blood of orks, their corpses
and body parts still wedged between chunks of rubble. The
ceiling had collapsed, letting the mid-afternoon sun lay
deep shadows across the proceedings.

'By what right were you sent into our forces?' demanded
Odaenathus.

'Is that really the issue, Chapter Master?' the Assassin
replied. He grimaced and took in a ragged breath. 'My
orders came directly from Lord Vangorich, in concert with
members of the Inquisition. Does it matter how or why? I
tell you again, I have seen inside the ork city. The force that
remains is overwhelming. Stronger than anything you have
yet encountered. You cannot attack.'

'Why did you not continue your mission to kill the Great
Beast?' asked Vulkan. 'Surely that was more important than
warning us of any danger. If you killed the target, our losses
become inconsequential.'

'I could not reach the Great Beast,' Esad Wire admitted
with a shake of the head. His eyes lost their focus for a few
seconds, seeing something that was only memory. 'I barely
breached the outskirts of its sanctum. It was even more luck
that I got out again. Tens of thousands of giant orks, armed
as well as your elite companies. But that is not the worst.

There is more than simply a warlord guiding this force. It is something far grander. A demagogue, a high priest perhaps.'

'An emissary of an *ork god*?' Bohemond spat the words, his fingers tight on the hilt of his sword. 'Folly! Do not attribute the trappings of civilisations to their primitive antics.'

'I have seen their temples and preachers,' the Assassin replied sharply, his gaze still moving from one Space Marine to the next, never stopping. Koorland noticed his defiant stare did not extend to Vulkan. 'I have witnessed the ceremonies, the rituals and sermons of their creed. This is holy war to the orks, every bit as zealous as that ill-fated, ridiculous Proletarian Crusade.'

'That changes nothing,' said Vulkan. 'If anything, it reinforces the importance of the Great Beast. If we slay the orks' demigod, we break them.'

'I agree,' said Wire. 'But I tell you without a word of a lie that we cannot reach the monster this way.'

'It's been baiting us the whole time,' Thane suggested, 'trying to draw us in at every turn. This last trap might be the final one.'

'It's an ork, it wants to fight,' Bohemond interjected. 'It is a smart ork. But do not give it more credit than that. It simply wants to fight on its own ground, its own terms.'

'We cannot let it,' said Koorland.

'It offers us no option, Lord Commander.' Vulkan stood up, as though about to leave. 'Must I say it yet again, you must have some faith, Koorland. If there is a single lesson I need you to learn, it is that there is no final defeat while you hold true to the service of the Emperor. We cannot give in to despair, no matter what happens. Even when it seemed that Horus could not possibly lose, those of us loyal to the Emperor continued to fight. Even when there was not even a vision of what winning might look like, we refused...'

Vulkan bowed his head. His voice trailed away, shoulders hunched by some personal, painful memory.

'We cannot out-brute the orks!' snarled Esad Wire. He lifted his hands imploringly. 'It is why we have lost every battle so far. It is why we will lose everything if we do not think harder rather than fight harder! Lord Vangorich sent me as his agent. Stop fighting a war and start thinking like Assassins!'

Bohemond growled something incoherent and Vulkan shook his head in disgust.

'You have a suggestion, *Assassin*?' asked Koorland.

'If you cannot get to the target, bring the target to you. Draw it out and then strike.'

'The Great Beast has resisted all military challenge so far,' said Vulkan, looking back at them. 'What could possibly draw it out of its fortress that we have not already done?'

'I've seen inside the palace.' The Assassin spoke quietly and quickly. 'Ullanor cannot sustain itself. If you think we must fight time as much as the enemy, the orks have it worse. They may have driven us from orbit, but not a single supply ship has landed in days. You see no sign of it here, but the warehouses, the great stores of the palace are virtually empty. Not even fresh water. Their supplies are so low, the orks are cannibalising each other. They've eaten all of the human slaves and started on their own. I saw the remains. The weak link in the chain is the need for support from the tribute worlds in the surrounding systems.

Ullanor's air and water are polluted, its food resources scarce.'

'Blockade is not an option, we need a swift victory too,' said Koorland. 'The ork relief armies will be upon us in three days at the most.'

'Then bring them to their knees in one,' said Esad Wire. 'Find the remaining stores and break them, whatever the cost.'

Vulkan returned, nodding. His demeanour had changed again, once more the resolute, proud warrior.

'Yes, that would work. Draw out the Great Beast and then we strike with everything.'

Koorland knew that it really would not be so simple, and was sure that the primarch was not naive either. But *faith* required a plan, no matter how hopeless.

A scrape of metal on stone and the hiss of pneumatics drew everyone's attention to the Cult Mechanicus representative – Magos Laurentis. The bizarre-looking tech-priest had listened to the exchanges without comment, but now stepped forward, limping slightly.

'If I might make a suggestion, commanders...'

CHAPTER SIXTEEN

Ullanor – high orbit

Thane strode off the ramp of the Thunderhawk, glad to feel the deck of the *Alcazar Remembered* beneath his boots again despite the grim circumstances and his immediate prospects of survival. Laurentis scuttled after him, chattering to himself in an irritating mix of Gothic and lingua-technis. The magos had expounded at length on the flight up to high orbit, regaling Thane with his outlandish theories on the brute-shield, the Great Beast and orkdom in general.

The Chapter Master was pleased to see Weylon Kale waiting for him beyond the opening flight deck doors.

'Shipmaster, please assimilate the targeting data carried by my companion and disperse the firing solutions through the fleet as itemised in the attendant records.' Thane waved Laurentis forward and the magos proffered a coil of cogitator tape which Kale took without comment. 'The fleet has manoeuvred as ordered?'

'It has, Chapter Master,' Kale replied, falling in beside his commander, jogging to keep up with Thane's long strides.

Laurentis clanked and clicked behind them, his head rotating rapidly from left to right and back as he took in his surroundings. 'But I do not understand. All scans show that the defensive field is still operational. If we move into attack range the orks will open fire, but the city is still protected.'

'Fluctuations, shipmaster,' said Laurentis. He accelerated to come alongside the officer. The tech-priest's head turned ninety degrees to regard Kale with his remaining eye. 'Study of the field when the first attack occurred has revealed that in order for weapons within the city limit to open fire, the field had to drop. It is not a one-way barrier! With the damage inflicted on the orks' capabilities, and further targeted strikes during the first window of opportunity, we have hypothesised that we can return fire within the temporal lapse of the protective layer.'

'*Return* fire?' Kale sounded dubious. 'We have to let them shoot at us first, Chapter Master? This is an untested hypothesis?'

'Yes,' said Thane. They reached a conveyor port and stopped. He looked at Kale, understanding the man's reluctance but in no mood for explanations or speeches. 'We cannot bring the field down in its entirety but we can do a lot of damage. As well as brute-shield projection sites and weapon positions, we will destroy much of the city's storage facilities, pipelines and energy grid. We will drive the orks out, even if it costs the fleet to do so.'

Kale said nothing else as they rode to the command bridge. He headed directly to the weapons consoles and then the vox-officers, handing over the carefully constructed attack solution prepared by Dominus Zhokuv and his best strategos. It maximised the amount of fire the ships would be able to pour down onto the city in the shortest time possible.

'We're ready, Chapter Master,' announced Kale. 'Commands have been transmitted and acknowledged.'

'Commence the attack, shipmaster,' Thane replied quietly.

The *Alcazar Remembered* powered on with the other surviving ships, a makeshift flotilla of Space Marine battle-barges and strike cruisers, Navy battleships, frigates and destroyers, Martian hemiolia and penteres. Several minutes passed before the Fists Exemplar flagship passed the invisible boundary that took them into range of the surface weapons. Another thirty seconds later and the call came from the augur array technicians.

'Targeting signals detected, Chapter Master. Multiple surface sources.'

'Ork void assets are incoming, Chapter Master,' another officer reported.

'Signal Admiral Acharya, he needs to keep those orks off our backs, whatever it takes,' replied Thane. 'All crew to firing stations, prepare for surface bombardment.'

He heard Kale mutter to himself as the shipmaster flexed his fingers into the sign of the aquila.

'Emperor protect us from the schemes of tech-priests...'

CHAPTER SEVENTEEN

Ullanor – Gorkogrod

The growl and grumble of hundreds of engines shook dust from the ruins. Exhaust fumes from the assembled tanks of the Astra Militarum swathed the rubble of Gorkogrod with an oily mist. Close to the front of the three columns of fighting vehicles – not right at the front, Field-Legatus Dorr knew well his place within the grander scheme of the plan – *Dorn's Ire* rumbled forward, accompanied by Leman Russ battle tanks, Chimera transports and Demolisher siegebreakers.

The deep red livery of Martian command vehicles broke the camouflage and grey of the Astra Militarum. Through the gloom strode the remaining Knights, ion fields gleaming, the rubble shifting and shuddering under their tread.

And last came the Titans, ponderous and magnificent, dwarfing even the war machines of the Knight Houses, their lamps shining like beacons in the pre-dusk gloom. The two Warlords led, followed by the Executor, flanked by the smaller Titans moving in echelon to the right.

War-horns sounded the challenge to the orks, a wave of sound that eclipsed all others for several seconds, shattering the last pieces of glass in broken windows, causing debris dunes to shift and tremble.

Dorr, sitting in the open hatch of the main turret to watch the awesome engines, covered his ears. He marvelled that he could feel the ground shake with each tread even through the bulk and vibration of the Baneblade.

Zhokuv advanced alongside the super-heavy tank, his piston-legged battle-rig carrying him easily over the broken ground. Further into the smog the remaining infantry forged through the broken city, some twenty-two thousand Imperial Guardsmen, skitarii, Space Marines and cybernetica. Dorr could see nothing of them, but knew they were there from the murmur of Galtan and the subalterns passing updates to each other on the command deck below.

Behind and above, the last few squadrons of Valkyries and Vultures, Lightnings, Thunderhawks, Marauders and other aircraft loitered just outside the range of the anti-air weapons that ringed the central citadel.

All was poised, the giant many-limbed and multi-headed creature that was the Emperor's war machine waiting for the moment to pounce.

'You know, for the first time since arriving on Ullanor, I actually think I know what we're doing,' Dorr confessed to Zhokuv. 'That we're all moving towards the same purpose now.'

No answer was forthcoming from Zhokuv. The dominus' reply was forestalled by a sudden flicker in the smog ahead. Green lightning raced across the clouds, illuminating the ruins with a jade glow. Watching this, Dorr's heart raced. Had the tech-priests' assertions been right?

With a last crackle of emerald fire, the brute-shield dropped.

Seconds later, before even a cry of triumph had left Dorr's lips, the sky erupted with missiles, las and coruscating blasts of energy racing up towards the void.

'Sound the charge!' Dorr dropped down into the turret, slamming the hatch closed. He wriggled past the gunners and through the accessway to the command deck.

'I'm glad I was never a tanker,' he muttered when he emerged into the space beyond, already nearly full with staff officers.

He almost fell into his chair as the *Dorn's Ire* gathered speed, the acceleration unexpected rather than rapid. The vox was alive with confirmations of the advance commencing, the voices of tank commanders and platoon officers, Titan Princeps and Knight Scions overlapping and competing. The surge of noise from the Baneblade's engines and the feeling of motion and power filled Dorr with urgent excitement.

'One way or another, by nightfall we'll know,' he told the others.

'Know what, field-legatus?' asked a subaltern.

'Whether we actually have a chance at killing the Great Beast.'

Valefor and his Blood Angels formed a red tip to the spear of the Imperial attack. Through circumstance and fortune, the warriors of Baal Secundus had suffered the least in the preceding battles, though they had still lost a quarter of the Space Marines that had arrived at Ullanor six days earlier.

Sergeant Marbas had fallen the day before, leaving only Rabael and Micheleus as the surviving members of the Sanguinary Guard. Their golden armour was much battered, patched by the Chapter Techmarines with raw grey ceramite and dull metal, the fibre bundles and servos exposed in places. Along with Valefor and his guard, Blood Angels Terminator veterans led the attack into the buildings under the shadow of the fortress-palace – a force of Space Marines that would punch through the ork defenders across a narrow front and turn behind them, trapping the aliens against the following column of Space Marine and Astra Militarum tanks. Elsewhere, other Chapters were doing likewise, piercing the defending army at several points to occupy them while the biggest war machines moved on the storage sheds and weapon silos.

Rockets flared up to the heavens and long cannons boomed out a storm of anti-orbital fire, their fury matched only by the descending ire of the fleet above. Lance strikes and plasma bolts fell upon Gorkogrod less than a kilometre from the Space Marine offensive, guided by signals from Scout squads and Land Speeders. Bombardment cannons on the Space Marine vessels unleashed thunderous salvoes against the ork city. The air-to-surface weapons of the Adeptus Astartes flattened entire blocks and warehouses, pulverised ramparts and towers, and immolated fuel depots and power stations with rare phosphex warheads.

Into the tempest charged the Blood Angels, the name of their primarch on their lips.

'*In memoriam Sanguinius!* We are the wrath, we are the vengeance!' cried Valefor, blade aloft. Sporadic small-arms fire flashed from the roof and upper windows of a cargo facility ahead. The burned-out remains of an orbital lifter sat on the flat landing pad beside the warehouse. A rocket sputtered past the Blood Angels captain and detonated against the Tactical Dreadnought armour of a following Terminator. The veteran shrugged off the blow without breaking stride, his storm bolter lifted to return fire with a blaze of bolts.

Smashing shoulder-first through the large metal freight door, Valefor led his Blood Angels inside.

The warehouse was all but empty – of supplies, at least. Hundreds of gretchin and orks crowded mezzanines and walkways, their fire suddenly engulfing the Blood Angels as they entered. Valefor fired back with precise, short bursts from his pistol while behind him the Terminators raked longer fusillades into the foe, the growl of storm bolters accompanied by the bass snarl of an assault cannon.

Valefor did not slow his run, heading directly into the knot of orks skulking around the last few crates and barrels at the back of the warehouse. His sword split the haft of an axe swung at his face while bolts from his pistol ripped out the wielder's chest. Bellowing the war cries of the Chapter, the last two Sanguinary Guard fell on the other orks. Jump packs howling, they leapt up to the upper gantries, crashing through the metal like ascending comets. Vambrace-mounted Angelus bolters chewed bloodily through the greenskins pouring down fire from above while their glaives parted bodies and limbs.

The Blood Angels continued on, erupting from the back

of the warehouse, pouring out across the street towards the next building. Even as the orks still alive inside the warehouse moved to follow, Predators and Land Raiders arrived, laying waste to the building with heavy weapons fire while Astra Militarum Valkyries and Ultramarines Land Speeders targeted the Blood Angels' next objective.

'Keep moving!' bellowed Valefor. Out in the open again he could see that the fire from orbit was less intense than just ten seconds earlier. Much of the ground fire had been silenced too, but the barrage from the starships was waning fast. A glance back confirmed a wave of Leman Russ and other Astra Militarum tanks bursting into the newly-seized streets, and behind them the far larger shadows of Knights and Titans loomed through the murk.

The blaze of immense guns flashed in the gloom. Habitation blocks and a large viaduct about three kilometres beyond the Blood Angels' right flank exploded with shell, plasma and volcano cannon impacts, collapsing and toppling in a plume of fire, smoke and dust. Valefor heard the cheers of the Imperial Guard half a kilometre behind as they swarmed into the breach made by his Space Marines.

He headed for the next building. After days of fighting over ruins, it seemed jarring to see intact walls, windows still glazed, doors and gates still barred. A row of tenements, factories and forts half a kilometre wide delineated the expanse between the extent of the Imperial force's previous attack and the crashing orbital fire. This was the line the Space Marines had to pierce before the brute-shield was restored. It was impossible to tell how many orks held those buildings, but Valefor's orders from the Lord Commander had been concise and clear – break through as swiftly as possible.

Debris from the smashed viaduct rained down as the Land Raider Crusaders forming the plunging fist of the Black Templars attack roared down the rubble-strewn streets of Gorkogrod. In the lead vehicle Bohemond listened to the bang and rattle of impacts on the assault carrier's upper armour, mixed with the higher-pitched ping of bullets.

'Do not think that the enemy target us without retort,' he voxed to his warriors, referring to the gauntlet of fire through which the column raced. Missiles and energy bolts screamed and whined around the five armoured transports. 'The stalwarts of the Astra Militarum shall see the Emperor's justice delivered to those that resist His divine will.'

The Crusader briefly left the ground as it sped over the remains of a collapsed wall, causing Bohemond to pause. He braced himself, waiting for the jarring impact of the seventy-tonne behemoth crashing down. Suspension and road wheels screeched in protest and the ten Space Marines sharing the compartment with him swayed in their restraints. Steadying himself against the firing cradle, where Adolphus manned the twin assault cannons atop the hull, Bohemond heard the gunner laughing.

'Joyous is the occasion on which we can deliver the Emperor's punishment,' the High Marshal continued, slapping Adolphus' leg. He pulled himself up to the roof cupola and slammed open the hatch. Seizing hold of the storm bolter mounted there, he added its fire to the raging storm from hurricane bolters, lascannons, heavy bolters and autocannons scything along the buildings to either side. 'Every bolt and blast is a rebuke by the Emperor! Every foe slain is vindication of our existence! Forget not that the Emperor Himself subjugated this world for mankind. Be mindful that noble Dorn himself, gene-father of Holy Sigismund, trod these lands.'

He rotated in the cupola, bringing the fusillade of bolts against a sandbagged gun position on the roof of a building ahead. The bags split and exploded, the orks behind them flung back by a tight cluster of detonations.

'We fight for ground no less sacred than that of Terra itself. Here the Triumph of Ullanor was held, to mark the greatest victory of humanity. That memory is tarnished, that victory undone by the foul greenskins that occupy this city. When we are done, when the Great Beast is slain and Holy Terra restored to renewed glory, a fresh Triumph shall be held in honour of the Master of Mankind, for His ire grants us success today. We follow in the steps of giants and shall not be judged poorly by it!'

CHAPTER EIGHTEEN

Ullanor – Gorkogrod

The anti-orbital barrage was sporadic – the few last rockets and the occasional pulse of crackling energy. Twelve minutes after the offensive had begun, the flash and boom from the last exchange of orbital fire dissipated. Three seconds later the brute-shield crackled back into life over Gorkogrod. Tank battles and firefights continued to rage below, but the Imperial line had been moved forward several kilometres to within direct-fire range of the outer palace fortifications.

Koorland headed to join the spearpoint of the attack in a Thunderhawk. Lascannon blasting, the heavy bolters unleashing their last rounds into the orks swarming away from the massive offensive, the gunship swept over central Gorkogrod. Koorland could see that the majority of the Imperial forces had moved inside the barrier. In particular the Titans and Knights were fighting at full effectiveness with void and ion shields intact.

Trails of broken tanks and flame-wreathed war engines marked the routes of attack, and in places he could see mounds of Astra Militarum dead and handfuls of bright Space Marine armour left in the wake of the quick advance. Smoking craters, ork corpses and partially collapsed buildings looked as if great claws had raked through the inner city towards the central palace-fortress.

The cost on the ground had been considerable, but lower than he had feared. He signalled the *Alcazar Remembered* and inquired after the success of the bombardment and status of the fleet.

'Eighty per cent of targets damaged or destroyed, Lord Commander,' replied Thane. 'I ordered the remains of the fleet to pull back to high orbit, it seemed pointless losing more ships for those last few storehouses.'

'I concur. Losses?'

'Severe.' Thane took a long, audible breath. 'Do you want the details, Lord Commander?'

'What sort of transport capacity is left, assuming that we can kill the Great Beast and get off this abominable planet?'

There was no reply for several seconds. Koorland hoped the delay was due to the need to gather the information rather than Thane's hesitation to break bad news.

'Dedicated Adeptus Astartes vessels could carry our remaining ground forces. Three thousand berths. Of the Imperial Navy, there's room for perhaps twelve thousand troops. Unsure regarding the Adeptus Mechanicus capacity. They have several Titan transports left that could house thousands but very little food and other supplies for soldiers.' Thane paused, leaving Koorland with nothing but static for a few seconds. 'Of course, given our losses on the ground, that's not really an issue any more, is it?'

'No,' the Lord Commander agreed. 'Very well, have the fleet prepared to conduct retrieval operations when needed. If Esad Wire's assessment is true, this will be a hard night for the orks. If it wants to maintain any control, the Great Beast will have to s–'

'Lord Commander!' The cross-force channel crackled with static from an emergency override. Koorland recognised Field-Legatus Dorr's voice. 'We have a new problem.'

He snapped his attention back to the city and needed no further explanation from the commander of the Astra Militarum. The centre of Gorkogrod was changing. Buildings and walls were folding, revealing massive portals opening into the ground.

From a thousand metres in the air Koorland had an almost perfect view, watching incredulously as large ramps opened in the ground to disgorge a tide of orks, fully armoured in plates of dull black, banners of the red fist flying above them.

They marched. Marched like the proudest Imperial Guardsmen. Dozens of massive battle tanks erupted from other enclosures, many-turreted monstrosities each the size of a Baneblade, their high-sided compartments carrying even more of the Great Beast's elite companies.

And dreadnoughts. And stompers. And gargants, some larger than the mighty Warlord and Executor Titans that were at the forefront of the Adeptus Mechanicus attack.

Parts of the city were also moving. Upward.

Like barges drifting away from their moorings, whole building tops detached themselves. Pulses of green light enveloped their undersides – more evidence of the advanced gravitic capacities the orks had somehow discovered. Koorland counted at least fifty of the hovering platforms.

The palace remained, squatting at the top of the mountain, the full extent of its walls and bastions revealed. From the angle of Koorland's view the entire complex looked like a single inter-linked construction, resembling nothing so much as a four-hundred-metre tall, crouching ork god carved in gigantic blocks of stone and skinned with metal plates.

Koorland could scarcely believe the sudden change in the city, and the sheer scale of the Great Beast's last reserves was breathtaking. But it was neither of these things that gave the Lord Commander a momentary pause. He had known of the giant orks from Esad Wire's testimony, though the reality was far greater than the threat. Koorland had witnessed first-hand the devastating new technologies of the orks, so it was not the weaponised city that struck him cold.

Two simple facts burned bright in his thoughts. The first was that the Great Beast had held back these forces despite the ruination of its city and the deaths of tens of thousands of its followers. The ruthlessness might be expected of any ork warlord, but the patience such a strategy betrayed was something no greenskin commander had ever previously demonstrated.

The second thought, the one that really made Koorland question the chances of victory, was that the Great Beast had recognised immediately the strategy the Imperial forces were enacting and had reacted with overwhelming force. The moment the first strikes had rained down on its supply depots the creature had known what Koorland and his army intended.

Just as at every stage since the commencement of the planetfall and assault, the Great Beast had simply been biding its time.

Gutting another foe, Bohemond noticed the ground trembling. At first he thought it was his Crusader's engine, but the *Sigismund's Pride* was stationary fifty metres behind the High Marshal, blasting its assault canons and hurricane bolters into the remnants of an ork gun pit.

'The Assassin was a liar,' spat Clermont as he hewed the head from another ork, its blood spattering against the life fluid of so many others drying on the castellan's armour. 'These warriors are no worthier foe than the scum we have slain for the past days!'

More orks spewed from the gutter-ramp ahead, their shrieks as wild as their firing. Bohemond and his guard met the fresh onslaught with bolters and blades, and for another few minutes the fury of close combat absorbed the thoughts of the High Marshal. It was a shout from Clermont that brought him out of his battle-trance to notice the wide shadow moving over the fallen buildings and corpse-choked street.

He looked up to see a massive platform floating impossibly over the ruined skyline, a hundred-metres-long oblong slab that gleamed with jade energy. On its back it carried five metal towers, and struts like gangplanks jutted from every level.

The hovering fortress slid to a halt a hundred metres

above Bohemond's force. Lascannon blasts from the Land Raiders flickered from its shimmering field. A circle opened in the centre of the bizarre engine, flaring with paler green light. A disc of energy descended from the opening, a crowd of heavily armoured orks clustered on the pulsing light as though it was a solid thing.

The Black Templars opened fire, bolters and heavy weapons strafing back and forth across the extending cylinder of light. From towers atop the construct emerged more armoured foes, the spark of power weapons and plasma chambers stark against the darkness of the flying keep. Brighter flares lit the sky as the orks jumped, falling down towards the Black Templars with green bursts of fire from their flight packs.

The drop-troops landed first, crashing into the Space Marines with bursts of plasma fire and sweeps of wickedly serrated power axes. Eddarin launched himself at them, several squads following his counter-attack.

The Black Templar hammered his chainsword against the raised power fist of a greenskin. His cry was of joy more than surprise. 'It's raining orks!'

If any servant of the Omnissiah or Emperor had doubted that the final battle for Gorkogrod had begun, those doubts were drowned by the growl of engines, the pounding of terrible cannons and the bellows of ten thousand gigantic mega-armoured orks.

The main cannon of the *Dorn's Ire* had run out of shells in the push across the boundary of the brute-shield, and it was reduced to lascannons and bolters against the incoming tide. The same was true of many of the field-legatus' super-heavy tanks, such had been the need for their guns in the prior days of battle. Normally they would have been resupplied by orbital drops, but any such action had been impossible given the lethality of the anti-orbital defences. Knights and Titans were not so limited, but the engines of the Adeptus Mechanicus were hard-pressed against the fresh surge of ork gargants and stompers.

'I fear these foes may be the match of us,' Dorr confided over his secure channel to Dominus Zhokuv. 'The damage was done with the first blow, and we simply don't have the guns to face these giants.'

'Your fear is ill-founded, field-legatus,' came Zhokuv's clipped reply. 'Trust ever in the artifices of the Machine-God to deliver us from harm.'

'We have already lost one of the Warlords and the other is beset by foes,' said Dorr.

'I speak not of Titans, but of a far newer addition to the arsenal of the Machine-God,' declared the dominus. 'If you would direct your attention a kilometre to the west...'

Dorr adjusted the auspex and vid-capture feeds to look at where the dominus indicated. Something enormous was advancing slowly through the rubble and shattered walls. It was longer than any of the ork sky-barges, carried on huge track units larger than battle tanks. Much of the superstructure was taken up with an immense cylinder surrounded by building-sized cabins and kilometres of scaffold and walkways.

'Are those...' Dorr looked again. 'Those tracks are from the *Praetor Fidelis*! What have you done to my Capitol Imperialis, Zhokuv?'

'The *Praetor Fidelis* has been given new life in a more functional form, field-legatus,' crowed Zhokuv. 'The reactors and tracks were very useful in my grand design. The weapon you might not recognise. We salvaged it from the wreckage of my forge-ship. A plasma accelerator.'

'You mounted a starship cannon on the bastardised remains of my command vehicle?' Dorr was not sure whether to cry or laugh. He opted for the latter.

'Behold the great device of the Omnissiah's retribution,' declared Zhokuv. 'Witness the power of the Machine-God's wrath. Pay homage to the mysteries of the Cult Mechanicus! Be in awe of the majesty of *Ordinatus Ullanor*!'

At the conclusion of the dominus' speech, the newly constructed Ordinatus opened fire. A scintillating stream of plasma blasts erupted from its weapon, striking the closest of the mega-gargants menacing the Imperial lines. Energies capable of overloading the defensive screens of voidships burst through the power fields of the gargant in moments. Energy shields parted in a collapsing shower of red lightning and green flares, the layers of fields evaporating in moments. The final blasts of the salvo tore through the gargant's plated shell – armour a tenth the thickness of a warship's hull.

Engines and ammunition detonated inside the brutal machine, scattering tank-sized debris and shrapnel through the mobs of orks marching in its shadow.

One minute and forty-five seconds later the Ordinatus

had recharged, its next target reduced to smoking slag by another fusillade of incendiary blasts.

'I'll light a hundred votives for the Omnissiah myself,' Dorr promised the dominus.

CHAPTER NINETEEN

Ullanor – central Gorkogrod

What is the point of an ork? What mishap of evolution or derangement of design would bring forth a creature entirely possessed of the need to conquer?

What purpose can it serve beyond destruction? And in such state it can serve no other purpose but its own eventual destruction.

Was that... Was there ever any future for us? Were we intended as nothing more than destroyers?

And at the end I become what I must. A beast to face a beast.

Blue lightning forked in all directions from the ork battle-tower. The psyker-carrying engine had been brought to a halt by the combined efforts of Rune Priest Thorild and two of his Librarius strike team, but the alien machine was proving difficult to finish off – not least because the background psychic presence of the orks still threatened to overload any human that tried to tap directly into the warp, limiting the psykers' strength.

'Khofus, draw out its spite,' the Space Wolf called to his companion from the Excoriators. His next words were directed to Epistolary Conneus of the Ultramarines. 'Use your power to shield Khofus from the worst. I will target the connection point.'

So instructed, the Librarians raced into action. Khofus stepped from the ruins and threw another blast of lightning at the weirdtower. Its psychic aura bulged outwards to form a green tentacle that lashed at the Excoriator. Khofus inverted his psychic draw, tapping into the stuff of the ork attack, fixing the lunging protrusion upon himself. As the green energies enveloped Khofus, Conneus threw his psychic might into the mind of his companion, bolstering the defences of his psychic hood to prevent the burning tendrils of orkish energy from burrowing into mind and flesh.

Thorild charged from cover, pushing his soul-fire into the head of his rune axe. The blade flared with blue light as he leapt up onto the structure of the immobilised tower and swung at the wavering tendrils of energy streaming from it. As the edge of the blade bit he let free his power, allowing it to surge into the ork psychic miasma.

A shock of feedback ran through him, body and soul, but he fought through the instant of pain and poured forth his rage. He let himself fall to the tossing sea that was the swelling of ork psychic potential into which the battletower tapped. Through that ocean of primal force pushed Thorild, just one of many swirls and counter-currents trying to break the immense tide.

As he moved against the churn of the current he noticed that all the energy was being drawn inward like an immense maelstrom, converging on a central point that was swelling with obscene power.

He let his psychic might explode in a devastating blast. His axe hewed through the intangible fabric of the tower's psychic aura and crashed through physical armour, slicing deep into the black-painted metal. The attack thundered through the machine and he leapt clear as psychic energy erupted with the howling of a wolf, tearing the ork contraption apart from the inside.

'Lord Commander,' he voxed, the image of the psychic tidal swell throbbing in his thought. 'Lord Commander!'

'Thorild, what is it?'

'Something is stirring in the palace. The Great Beast, I think. The ork psychic potential is accumulating massively. It will not be long before...'

Koorland did not catch the end of the message as the Space Wolf's voice trailed away. Over the jutting ruins, the Lord Commander saw something immense moving up from the centre of the city.

'I see it too, Rune Priest.'

At first it looked as though the entire palace had risen. After a moment, Koorland realised it was just the central portion, what he and the others had taken to be a temple. It was like the gargants in shape, a bulky, rotund idol, but so much larger in size as to defy belief. Gravitic projectors and thundering jets lifted the edifice above the surrounding buildings. It was so much larger than any war machine the orks had sent before that it defied the senses, blotting out the setting sun with its bulk.

Guns and rocket batteries studded its surface, along-side dish-shaped gravity weapons and outlandish energy cannons. Fluctuating fields encased the black-and-white behemoth. What appeared to be a dome pushed upwards, revealing itself as a grimacing ork face wrought in plates of riveted metal and smooth stone.

Buildings crumbled under the wash of energy. The city turned to dust like a bow wave before the advance of the titanic effigy-machine. Thunderhawks, Valkyries and Lightnings swooped and fired, their missiles, shells and bullets coursing across the temple-gargant's fields, leaving after-sparks of dissipating power but nothing more. Hastily redirected artillery boomed out, rocket batteries and guns throwing their devastating weight against the onslaught of the Great Beast's mobile fortress. Like the air strikes, they achieved nothing save to engulf the citadel in a curtain of emerald power.

A few kilometres away, *Ordinatus Ullanor* roared its anger again. A hail of plasma bolts smashed into the temple-gargant. Fields crackled and spat, but the construct continued to advance unblemished.

The vox crackled with another transmission from Thorild.

'Lord Commander, I can feel the hate building. I think the temple-gargant is about to unleash s–'

Again his warning came too late. The eyes of the temple-gargant lit with pale green force. Twin beams of dazzling power lashed across the city, running the length of *Ordinatus Ullanor*. Plasma chambers exploded, turning the Adeptus Mechanicus engine into an artificial sun that engulfed an area half a kilometre across, turning buildings, men and orks to vapour.

'We can't stop it,' Koorland whispered. 'We have no defence against that kind of power.'

From amidst a sea of greenskin bodies, Vulkan watched the emergence of the sanity-defying ork engine. The sky burned with the impacts of rockets, shells and las-blasts, surrounding the floating temple with a star-like corona. Its eyes gleamed as the main weapon recharged while torrents of fire streamed down from scores of emplacements and heavy cannons.

The Great Beast had sent its best and now it had been forced to reveal itself.

The primarch smiled.

Soldiers of the Imperium died by the thousand and fled the Great Beast's wrath in even greater number. Agents and artifices of the Omnissiah were worthless against the might of the orks' mechanically rendered god. Titans and Knights fell before the crushing power of the temple-gargant. Those Martians and their subject troops with the will to retreat did so. The tech-priests and cybernetica held fast, even against the overwhelming logic of withdrawal, constructed or engineered by choice or intervention to respond only to the commands of their overlords. Dominus Zhokuv would see the affront against the Machine-God destroyed or else be destroyed himself in the effort.

Dorr did his best to maintain a line against the encroachment of the massive war-edifice. His tanks pounded the last of their shells into its armoured belly as it swept overhead, while the infantry battalions left to him battled to resist fresh waves of armoured orks discharged from keeps on its flanks. Having fought so hard to reach the temple, now it came for them and there was nothing they could do but dig in and die fighting.

The Space Marines attacked.

Koorland rode with Vulkan in the lead Storm Eagle, along with Thane, Bohemond and their attendant retinues.

'As then, so now,' said the primarch. If not actually enjoying the blooms of anti-aircraft fire, the clatter of shrapnel on the hull and the whine of air across the cracked canopy, he was certainly invigorated by the circumstances, more focused than at any time since their arrival.

'As when, lord primarch?' asked Koorland.

'The Great Crusade, of course,' replied the gene-father of the Salamanders. 'Or the Heresy Wars. And the Scouring. Not since those days have our brothers been tasked with such a momentous labour, nor responded with such ferocity.'

'Like old times?' suggested Thane.

'Exactly that.'

Squadrons of other gunships packed with the surviving warriors of the Adeptus Astartes followed, along with dozens of transports and support craft commandeered from the Imperial Navy and Astra Militarum. Each was filled to capacity with Space Marines. Below them assault troops bounded forward with jump pack-assisted leaps, crashing through the remaining ork resistance. Land Speeders of many patterns with more Space Marines clinging to their sides wove through the desolation. All that had survived the fighting thus far converged on the Great Beast's last bastion.

Fists Exemplar, Black Templars, Soul Drinkers, Ultramarines, Executioners, Dark Angels, Crimson Fists, Excoriators, Salamanders, Space Wolves, Blood Angels. And one Imperial Fist.

In all the panoply of a dozen Chapters, the last three thousand heroes of the Adeptus Astartes launched their final assault.

CHAPTER TWENTY

Ullanor – temple-gargant sanctum

Momentum. Direction. Ruthless aggression. These are the true weapons of the victorious. Hesitation is defeat.

And we hesitated. When the guns of our brothers roared, shock laid the first blow. We were lax and they were not. The war lasted seven years, but the dream was destroyed in that first second. What was left worth fighting for after? Pride. Foolish pride.

Caestus assault rams that Koorland had kept in reserve now flew past the lead transports in the final seconds before contact with the objective. Their melta charges and reinforced prows smashed through the walls of the temple-gargant in blasts of super-heated air and vaporised metal. Squads deposited within the structure pushed into the waiting foe with blades, bolters and grenades, forcing beachheads fifty metres into the mechanical behemoth.

Volleys of fire from the gunships raked across the mobs of orks crowding the surface of the war machine, rockets and bullets flaring up towards them as they descended. A few Imperial Navy fighters and bombers flew final passes above and below the focus of the Space Marine attack, plasma-tipped missiles and heavy bolters incinerating and shredding even more defenders. Turrets spat torrents of shells and las-blasts, exacting a deadly toll for the bravery of the crews.

In rapid waves the Space Marine gunships despatched their cargoes into the breaches created by the assault rams, while ad hoc transports deposited more squads into the ramparts and walkways of the temple-gargant's exterior to seize conventional ingress points.

Koorland kept close to Vulkan. The primarch did not pause for a moment, his hammer in constant motion as he waded into the orks crewing the temple-gargant. Mega-armour shattered under the blows, power claws and energy blasts bouncing from the ancient war-plate forged by his hand.

Koorland had a little time to take stock of his surroundings, and was surprised by what he saw. He had expected the usual ork technology – clanking pistons and gears, hissing steam pipes, the stench of oil and corroded metal.

Instead the interior of the temple-gargant was almost pristine. The walls were chrome-like, painted with friezes of simple black and white dags or check patterns. Embossed plates of glyphs marked many doorways and junctions – signs, he realised with some shock. Doors slid open with faint purrs. The lights were a pale blue with barely a flicker of power flow.

In fact there seemed to be very little in the way of outward energy sources. Everything hummed and gleamed with its own radiant light, the same strange power that fuelled all of the new ork technology.

He had little enough time to process the importance of this observation. The needs of the mission were far more pressing.

Hundreds of Space Marines forced their way into the hovering edifice, charging into brutal combat with the Great Beast's monstrous elite. Terminators and Dreadnoughts led the assault in many places, their heavier armour weathering the fire of the orks to allow their power-armoured brothers to gain a foothold, weapons filling the corridors and chambers with continuous hails of fire.

There were few foes that survived the charge of Vulkan, but many adjoining corridors and halls spilled forth their own flood of raging greenskins as the primarch thrust fast towards the heart of the impossible war engine. Armed and armoured with the best from the slave-lines of Ullanor's manufactories, these creatures were as deadly as Esad Wire had warned.

Yet they were confronted at the fore by seven Chapter Masters and twice as many more Space Marines of high rank and great prowess. Many of Vulkan's companions carried artefacts dating back to the Heresy Wars and earlier – swords, hammers, maces and shields that first saw battle during the Great Crusade and even the Unification Wars. They cut down the orks with plasma pistols, volkite carbines and thermal blasters forged on Mars before any of their Chapters had been founded. And each warrior was already a renowned hero amongst his brothers, his life a succession of great victories and campaigns that would grace future

rolls of honour. Their names and titles would be lauded by generations to come.

Koorland felt humbled by such company, but in that time of unrelenting madness, a seeming eternity in which he waded into a sea of screaming ork faces, he finally understood the meaning of Vulkan's assertions.

He had faith.

In himself. In the choice of the primarch to take him as his heir-in-command, above all others present.

And he had faith in his battle-brothers. If ever a band of warriors could triumph against the odds ranged against them, they had been gathered here. If there were any weapon in the armoury of the Imperium that Koorland could choose to wield at that moment, it would be three thousand warriors of the Adeptus Astartes.

And, lastly but most keenly, he had faith in Vulkan. The primarch was a vital energy every bit as powerful as the one against which they were set. Perhaps it was destiny or some other impulse that drove Vulkan, but whatever the cause he seemed set on a course and knew exactly where to lead them.

Into the depths of the temple-gargant, racing towards a confrontation with the Great Beast.

They came upon a large hall at least two hundred metres long and thirty high. Here the lights were dimmed, a respectful ochre that bled orange shadows behind the advancing Space Marines. The greater part of the force had created a cordon and held back the ork counter-attack while Vulkan, Koorland and their companions, accompanied by a mixed-Chapter company two-hundred strong including the cadre of Librarians, pressed ahead for the final assault on the Great Beast.

The sides of the hall were piled with detritus several metres deep. Tattered cloth, bent metal spars and splintered wooden poles made strange shapes in the gloom. The footfalls of the Space Marines echoed from the metallic walls and ceiling, loud against the backdrop of weapons fire resounding through the corridors behind.

'What is this?' asked Thane, moving to one of the trash piles. He pulled free a piece of cloth several metres long. He turned it, a richly embroidered sheet slashed and burned, golden thread glimmering in the light. Words were stitched into the design, human words, above a double-headed eagle. 'It's the aquila. By the Emperor...'

All of the rubbish was made of broken standards, torn and hacked and desecrated by the orks. Metal eagles and lightning bolts adorned some of the poles, bent and hammered out of shape.

'From the Triumph,' growled Vulkan, ripping free a rag of banner. It bore the icon of the Blood Angels Legion.

'I know this design,' he whispered. 'It was the personal banner of Captain Nemedeus. I knew him from the Artagean campaign. His whole company died during the Ullanor assault.'

Valefor rushed forward and laid a hand reverently upon the cloth. 'One of our greatest sacrifices. I bear his sword still!'

They continued past the broken, heaped remains of mankind's last victory over the orks of Ullanor. The far end of the hall was not a wall but two immense doors fashioned from grey and black marble into a grimacing ork face, layered with precious metals studded with gems.

'The breaking of the banners, I understand,' said Quesadra. 'But this kind of ornamentation is not in the aesthetic of the orks.'

'Look at the floor,' added Koorland. 'It is polished granite.'

'From the parade ground along which the victorious armies of the Emperor marched,' said Vulkan. He gestured towards the doors as they neared. 'And doubtless this is from some other structure associated with the Triumph.'

Koorland thought the primarch sounded wistful.

'The high point of the Great Crusade,' Vulkan continued. 'The culmination of decades of war. The beginning of the end, we used to think. But we did not realise what that meant, how true those words would be. Such hope, such greatness, was the height from which we fell. Here we built the tallest pinnacle before the deepest drop. If only the orks knew what ruin they wrought here.'

He fell silent, and in the absence of his voice the hall gently rang with the retort of weapons in the surrounding corridors and chambers.

'An attempt at humiliation,' said Bohemond. 'An empty gesture.'

'An assertion of power,' Vulkan corrected him, 'stated by the Great Beast to its own kind. When we slay it, our statement will be louder still.'

When the Space Marines were halfway down the hall a shudder rumbled through the chamber. Two broad portals slid open, one on each side of the gateway. Metallic clanks and thudding steps heralded the arrival of a pair of identical stompers. They were fashioned as grotesque caricatures of orks, rotund mechanical beasts with guns and saw-blades for arms, the head of each almost scraping the high ceiling. They were painted in red and black with splashes of bright yellow, festooned with Titan kill-banners looted from the display of the Ullanor Triumph. Koorland recognised the icon of the ancient and honoured Fire Wasps Legio.

Koorland barked orders even as the machines opened fire. The Space Marines split, Vulkan and one contingent heading for the engine on the right, Koorland and the rest to the stomper on the left.

An explosion engulfed three battle-brothers while large-calibre rounds screamed through half a dozen more. Bolts flared through the dim light, a storm of small detonations wreathing each war machine.

Koorland fixed his attention on the target ahead, trusting to Vulkan to deal with the other mechanical giant. Eye-like lamps blazed into life and its head turned towards him, as though specifically seeking him out. He could see ork crew loitering on the shoulder gantries, firing their side-arms while the massive gun of the right arm adjusted aim amongst much gear-grinding and chain-rattling.

'Melta bombs!' he cried, taking a fist-sized charge from his belt.

The stomper's main cannon roared again, flame and fury engulfing more of the Space Marines just behind Koorland. His armour registered the wash of heat from the detonation but he ignored the amber warning flashes.

The stomper took a step, exhaust smoke billowing as

engines rumbled. It swung its right arm, a wicked chain-blade thrice as long as Koorland was tall. The whirring teeth snarled over the Lord Commander's head. He heard the snap of shattering ceramite and a cry from Quesadra.

Glancing back Koorland saw the blade sweep on and up, bloodied teeth hurling chunks of the bisected Chapter Master across the black granite and vandalised banners. The Crimson Fists shouted their dismay and swore vengeance, the blood of their commander spattered on their armour as they charged the ork engine.

Nearing the stomper, Koorland sheathed his blade and jumped, his fingers finding purchase on the metal belly plates of the ork war machine. The metal clanged around him as others landed on the towering engine, smashing at the armour with power fists and thunder hammers, with the more staccato chime of maglocks as melta bombs were slammed into place.

Koorland pulled himself up a few more metres, to where a viewport was cut into the plates. A diminutive gretchin stared out in horror. He plunged his fist into the war machine's chest and dragged the creature out of the hole. Activating the melta charge's timer, he tossed the bomb into the stomper's interior and pushed away, jumping down to the hall floor.

He had time to glance across the hall, to see Vulkan emerge from the smoking ruins of the other engine, fumes coiling around the glowing head of Doomtremor, his war-plate smeared with oil and alien gore.

The melta bombs detonated in a rippling cascade over a few seconds, turning the stomper's metal hide into showers of molten drops, slashing through the mechanisms within with blasts of super-heated gas. Fuel stores and ammunition ignited, ripping the stomper apart with secondary detonations. The Space Marines withdrew as jagged debris and burning hunks of ork flesh rained down onto them.

Vulkan was already at the gate, standing before the portal with Doomtremor held aloft ready to strike.

Before he even started to swing his weapon, a line of light appeared between the doors and the portal swung away, opening inwards to the sanctum beyond, flooding the outer hall with bright, pale green light.

Koorland and the others followed the primarch over the threshold, weapons ready. Koorland checked on his small force. About a third had fallen to the stompers' attack. He could hear fighting from beyond the hall, getting closer. The rearguard was collapsing.

The chamber past the gateway was most definitely a power generator of some kind. Koorland was reminded of the plasma chambers of Imperial fortresses and starships, the walls lined with pipes and crackling cables, in this instance thick bundles of coppery wire strewn like garlands that hissed and sparked with green energy. The air throbbed with latent power. Koorland could feel the vibrations through his armour.

But it also put him in mind of the Ecclesiarchy shrines. Past the mechanical aspects, the walls had the same decorations as much of the rest of the temple-gargant – glyph plates and stark mosaics, painted geometric designs and pictorial murals. The chamber was semicircular, about thirty metres across, the focus of the arrangement an ork idol sitting upon an ornate chair.

The statue was at least ten metres tall, in a square-arched alcove filled with the green light of ork power. Its body was encased in thick layers of plate, intricately wrought and carved with orkish designs. A bull-horned helm with a mock tusked face encased the head. Two claws each the size of a Space Marine rested on the arms of the chair.

'Master of Terra...' muttered Odaenathus.

'Speak not of the Throneworld in this place,' growled Bohemond. 'What further mockery is this?'

A plethora of cables hung from the armoured form of the idol, fizzing with power. It was clear that the statue was the centre of the power generation system, though by what means Koorland did not know. He looked to the Rune Priest, Thorild.

'Is this the centre of the psychic presence?'

'The power of the waaagh suffuses this place,' replied the Space Wolf, with some evident effort, his voice strained. 'It is both the vortex and the sun, the consumer and the creator.'

Koorland looked sharply at the psyker, remembering the ork-possession that had beset some of the other Librarians. The Space Wolf seemed in control of himself, merely being poetic in his choice of words.

'Let us destroy the reactor and find the Great Beast,' declared Thane, stepping towards the energy-shrouded god-effigy.

'Where are you?' Bohemond called, stalking after the Exemplar. 'False priest to an artificial god! No Great Beast here, just alien impostors!'

The air buzzed with a surge of power. An inhuman shriek echoed around the chamber and all eyes turned to Thorild, the source of the terrible cry. He shuddered, lightning arcs of green power spewing from his psychic hood, his rune-staff burning with jade flames. Moments later the other Librarians collapsed, screaming in most un-Space Marine fashion, cries of utter terror and agony ripped from them.

Gandorin staggered wildly, flares of green sparks arcing from his helm. He stopped a few metres from Koorland, face twisted in a terrifying snarl. A second later his head exploded, showering brain matter and skull across the Lord Commander.

Disgusted, Koorland turned on the idol as the smoking corpses of the psykers clattered to the floor. Bohemond roared, the chains binding his sword to his wrist rattling as he raised his weapon in challenge.

'Face us, coward! Your death has arrived, false prophet of a doomed race. Ullanor shall be razed again, and none shall remember the Great Beast.'

With a drawn-out creak, the statue stirred.

Bohemond took a step back.

Koorland felt the other Space Marines crowding closer as the idol's eyes became stars of green fire. He looked away and his grip loosened on his weapons, and it was only when he felt the presence of Vulkan looming up beside him that he was able to look at the animating effigy again. The primarch stood with legs slightly apart, hammer held up like a shield.

Power flared and pipes hissed while cables and wires detached from the idol with fountains of emerald sparks. Clanking and whirring, the immense machine rose up from its throne and took a step out of the alcove, twice as tall even as Vulkan.

'We destroyed your other engines,' said Thane, brandishing his sword. 'This will be no different.'

Koorland looked up at the living idol, filled with foreboding. Black and white checks adorned the effigy, the face painted a deep red. At its full height, the thing seemed even bigger, swamping the primarch with its bulk, a monster of moulded plates and jutting spikes covered with writhing, coiling fronds of power.

'It isn't a war machine,' Koorland told the others, the words almost choking him. 'It's a suit of armour.'

CHAPTER TWENTY-ONE

Survival begets sacrifice. How long have You sat immobile, my Father? They speak in Your name and know nothing of Your mind. Is this what You wanted? I cannot countenance such a thing. It is a travesty of the Imperial Truth, the epitome of all that we wished to vanquish. Venal, selfish, corrupted. Did we not show the way brightly enough? Did our blood not wash the wounds clean?

Why do You not speak out? Father, why have You forsaken me?

'The Great Beast must die, whatever the cost.'

The last words to leave Odaenathus' lips were painfully prescient. The Great Beast threw out a flame-wreathed fist and a blast of power smashed into the Ultramarines Chapter Master, smearing his remains across several metres of granite. For a couple of seconds, Koorland couldn't drag his eyes from the droplets of molten armour and the stain of blood-grease that had been his fellow commander. All that he was, all that he might be, had been ended with contemptuous ease.

Koorland looked again at the Great Beast, a manic laugh threatening to burst free as he considered the impossibility of taking on such a foe.

'Destroy the generator,' snapped Vulkan. He stepped past, hefting Doomtremor in one hand. 'Orks love to fight. I'm going to give the Great Beast exactly what it wants.'

The tone of the primarch left Koorland no choice – a command that reached into his heart and head and could not be gainsaid. Even had he the inclination to defy Vulkan, he had no time. The gene-father of the Salamanders threw himself at the gargantuan ork, his hammer a blue star against wreathing clouds of green fire.

At Koorland's command the remaining Space Marines poured fire into the arcane technology of the reactor. Bolts, volkite flares and melta bursts rippled across the screen of shimmering energy that covered the mass of machinery surrounding the Great Beast's throne. The green curtain broke into constellations of small stars, rippling and surging with energy flux.

'More!' roared Koorland, loading a new magazine into his pistol. The juddering snarl of assault cannons and bark of bolters drowned out the boom of Doomtremor striking the Great Beast's armour and the shriek of power claws raking across Vulkan's war-plate. The converging fire of the taskforce was a near-solid stream of energy and metal. The reactor field writhed and buckled, building to blinding intensity, but did not break.

Vulkan and the Great Beast reeled to one side and then

the other, smashing titanic blows against each other. Sparks and lightning fountained from the plate of both warriors. Their movement exposed the throne alcove of the reactor.

'There is another way,' declared Valefor. He dashed past the melee between the two behemoths and slashed his sword against the brute-shield. Green-black energy flared, throwing the Blood Angel twenty metres, his plate ripped apart. Koorland suppressed a cry of woe, his grief tempered by a slight movement from the crippled Blood Angel.

'He still lives!' one of Valefor's warriors declared, kneeling beside the fallen hero.

How long do any of us have? Koorland wondered, looking at the ongoing struggle between the Great Beast and Vulkan. In the presence of such demigods, what worth were the efforts of simple mortals?

Taking up Doomtremor in both hands, the primarch ducked beneath a swinging strike from the Great Beast and threw all of his weight behind his next blow. The head of the hammer crashed against the thigh of the immense ork, the thunderous sound of the blow lost amidst a deafening bellow of pain. The Great Beast staggered, a lightning-tipped claw lashing out to rip across Vulkan's chest, peeling apart the outer layer of his plastron.

The Great Beast recovered almost immediately, warding away the primarch's next blow with an upraised arm. It kicked hard, a monstrous foot connecting with Vulkan. The impact sent the lord of the Salamanders spinning away, his chestplate buckled even more.

'Target the ork!' shouted Thane, turning his weapon on the Great Beast.

The fusillade of the Space Marines engulfed the warlord with the same intensity as the reactor. And with similar lack of effect. Vulkan staggered to his feet, ripping away his broken plastron to reveal a layer of banded armour beneath.

The Great Beast turned to face the primarch. It raised a hand and beckoned mockingly with a finger.

'Lord Koorland!' Vulkan circled, moving his hammer to the left then the right, adjusting his stance constantly to mask his next attack. The Great Beast stepped and turned, keeping the primarch and Space Marines in view.

'My lord?' Koorland advanced, weapons at the ready.

'Leave! If I cannot end this here, none of us can. I know what to do, but it will be the end of us all if you stay. You must survive. You are the Imperial Fists, the Last Wall. And you are Lord Commander. Do not let the High Lords squander our victory, nor make vain my sacrifice.'

Over the crackle of the generator and the thud of the Great Beast's steps Koorland could hear shouts – ork and human – echoing along the outer hall. The sound of gunfire and crashing blows was almost in the hall itself. He looked at the primarch, and then to the immensity of the Great Beast.

Could Vulkan possibly prevail?

And he remembered Vulkan's assertions since the beginning. Faith, belief, the importance of symbols. He, Koorland, was the sole survivor of Ardamantua, the Lord Commander and heir to the likes of Dorn and Guilliman.

And he realised that Vulkan had known this moment would come from the time he had first heard of the Great Beast. An immovable object required an unstoppable force to match it. Neither primarch nor warlord could prevail.

But that was not Vulkan's plan.

Koorland looked at the primarch, his massive frame rendered to mortal proportions by the immensity of his foe. It was more than size alone that gave Vulkan his power. Into him the Emperor had put every artifice and effort to create the most sublime warrior – a figure of imagination and myth as much as brute strength.

Intellect beyond Koorland's understanding guided that power. A mind that had witnessed all of the glories and horrors of the galaxy through nearly two millennia of constant war.

A warrior who had seen his gene-sons slaughtered by their battle-brothers, who had taken up arms against his own brother demigods for the Emperor.

What could Koorland know of an immortal's mind and reasoning?

Vulkan perhaps sensed the attention of the Lord Commander. He looked at Koorland with eyes that had seen more than any other human soul. What was it Koorland saw in them? Pain? Yes, but not of the physical kind, not from the marks upon armour and flesh. It was the agony of wisdom. An ache of many centuries.

And in that gaze Koorland came to know what Vulkan had always known, and saw the intent of the Emperor's last loyal son.

The Great Beast roared, a deafening wall of sound matched by a flare of power rippling through the generator crackle. The glow of the warlord's claws brightened and became flames. Vulkan swung his hammer again, fending off the next blow. A tempest of sparks erupted where weapons clashed.

'All forces, evacuate the objective,' Koorland announced over the command vox. 'Immediate fighting withdrawal from the temple-gargant.'

Most of his companions started towards the doorway. The Blood Angels heaved up Valefor and carried him from the chamber. A score or so of the Space Marines stayed where they were. Black Templars.

Bohemond moved in the opposite direction, blocking Koorland's path.

'What fresh insanity is this?' spat the High Marshal, barely audible over the tumult of Vulkan and the Great Beast. 'The lord primarch needs us.'

'He does not,' Koorland answered calmly. He stepped to go past the Black Templar. Bohemond grabbed the Lord Commander's arm.

'We swore to die for the Emperor. We do not retreat! We are not cowards!'

Koorland's fist hit Bohemond square in the faceplate. The blow knocked the High Marshal crashing to the floor. The other Black Templars took steps towards their commander, blades and bolters raised.

'*I am your Lord Commander!*' The rage boiled from Koorland, allowed free vent after so much loss and frustration. No more could he withstand the jibes and barbs of the Black Templar's scorn. The endorsement of the lord primarch was enough. Koorland no longer cared for the affirmation of Bohemond and could certainly not spare the thought or effort required to continue seeking it. He pointed the tip of his blade at the downed warrior. 'Refuse me again and your life is forfeit, by my hand or word.'

Bohemond lay where he had fallen, shamed. Koorland turned his back on the High Marshal and strode away.

'If you want to die, stay here. If you want to serve the Emperor, come with me.'

CHAPTER TWENTY-TWO

Ullanor – Gorkogrod

There was never an external threat to mankind that we could not overcome. The greatest foe always lies within. That is the only lesson to be learned. No matter how bleak times become, the power to prosper or fall is held in the breast of every man and woman. The chain is as strong as the weakest link, but mankind has the Emperor to bear the weight of all. And it was from within that the deadly blow was dealt. Deadly. A lingering death, fifteen hundred years of slow pain. How much longer until the corpse admits its demise? Longer than I can bear to witness any more.

Forget the power of technology and science, for so much has been forgotten, never to be re-learned. Forget the promise of progress and understanding, for there is only war. There is no peace amongst the stars, only an eternity of carnage and slaughter, and the laughter of thirsting gods.

The Great Beast was an elemental force. Vulkan could feel the pressure of its power lapping against him like heat, an embodiment of the raw and raging instincts of the orks. Although he remembered little of his almost ceaseless labours against the daemons of the Dark Gods during the Heresy War, the primarch recalled enough to know that one did not win such a fight. It was victory merely to sustain it.

He caught a claw with the haft of Doomtremor, muscles and armour fibre-bundles straining against the warlord's brutal strength. Vulkan shifted his weight, widening his stride as he heaved off the Great Beast's next attack, moving quickly to his other foot to avoid the monstrous ork's return swing. He smashed Doomtremor against the greenskin's armour, its fire-shrouded head bouncing from energy-charged plates.

'In your ignorance, do you see what you have wrought?' Vulkan said, swinging his hammer again. 'Your kind should have stayed dead where we buried you.'

They exchanged more blows. Vulkan struggled to keep his footing against the hammering impact of every strike, but slowly circled to his left, manoeuvring the ork into position.

'You moved too soon,' Vulkan continued. 'Had you but the patience of true intelligence you would have seen that another decade, perhaps two, and the Imperium would have crumbled easily. And to strike at the Throneworld... You have roused a different beast, one that will see you crushed.'

The Great Beast surprised him. It did not draw back its fist, but reached out and snatched him by the throat. War-plate groaned under the pressure of the ork's fierce grip, tightening around Vulkan's windpipe. He rained blows against its arm as the warlord pulled back its other fist for a blow that would take off the primarch's head. As the claw powered towards his face, Vulkan switched the focus of his attack, slamming Doomtremor into the oncoming fist.

The explosion of competing powers parted the two combatants, flinging Vulkan into the wall and sending the Great Beast staggering across the floor, spiked boots gouging furrows in the stone.

The ork shook its arm and hand, numbed by the impact. Vulkan blinked hard to clear his spinning vision.

'But you are not the real threat,' the primarch snarled, pushing to his feet. He spun Doomtremor in his palms, sizing up his opponent. 'You are the distraction that will allow the true enemy to surge forth again.'

The two giants hurled themselves at each other. The Great Beast crushed the bodies of fallen Chapter Masters underfoot. Vulkan threw Doomtremor at the last moment, casting the burning hammer into the Great Beast's face. Armour buckled and split and the hammer whirled away across the chamber.

Vulkan wheeled past the stunned ork, but not so swiftly that he avoided its next punch, which caught him square in the gut and launched him a dozen metres through the air. Turning his crash into a roll, Vulkan regained his feet.

Its helm was a mess, but the ork now stood between the primarch and his weapon.

The flames around one of the Great Beast's gauntlets flickered away. It reached up and tore free the remnants of its helmet, tossing the mangled armour aside. Its head was enormous, with tusks and fangs like swords. The Great Beast regarded Vulkan with deep red eyes, a permanent scowl furrowing its brow.

'You are right, son of the Emperor,' it said. The voice was deep, guttural, but unmistakably speaking Imperial Gothic.

Vulkan was so taken aback by this utterance that he barely dodged the blast of power that erupted from the Great Beast's out-thrust fist.

'Your empire is on its knees. We shall be its death.' The Great Beast glanced over its shoulder and turned back to the primarch with what Vulkan believed was a smile. 'And just like your Emperor, you have thrown away your most powerful weapon.'

The Great Beast lowered its head and charged with a roar, green flames bursting from its fists. Vulkan leapt aside and threw a hand out towards Doomtremor, activating the miniature teleport link he had fitted into its head and his gauntlet. With a crack of splitting air, the hammer appeared in his fist. He swung hard, aiming for the side of the Great Beast's head.

The blow bounced from thick skull, Doomtremor's power field ripping skin and flesh down to the bone, searing a streak across the Great Beast's scalp.

The ork lumbered away. A pulse of power flooded from it in a shockwave, staggering Vulkan as he readied for his next strike.

The Great Beast straightened, thick blood pouring down its face, a visible crack in the side of its skull.

'Are you feeling tired yet, son of the Emperor?' it asked. Green coils of energy snaked up to its face, flowing over the wound, healing the gash in a few seconds. The Great Beast laughed. 'Is that the hardest you can hit me?'

'I don't have to hit harder,' Vulkan replied. 'I just have to think quicker.'

Their last exchange had brought the Great Beast back in front of the massive throne alcove in the heart of the reactor. The primarch hurled himself full force, tackling the warlord in the midriff to take them both into the pulsating green aura of the energy field.

At the moment of entry, Vulkan felt the overwhelming nature of Ullanor pouring into him. He witnessed and participated in the unimaginable orkishness of Ullanor, feeling himself drawn out into a web of waaagh power stretching across many star systems, the pulsing tendrils feeding back into his being even as his presence radiated energy into those around him.

That power echoed back through time, past the Horus Heresy to the primordial origins of the orks themselves. He was one with the nature of the orks, and saw for the briefest moment two green-skinned behemoths battering each other with bare fists at the dawn of time before even mankind was born.

The sensation of something around his throat dragged Vulkan back to the present, staring into the rage-filled eyes of the Great Beast. Both claws were on his throat, squeezing the life from the primarch.

Having seen the nature of the waaagh-force that bound the orks together, guessing at its nature from his own dark experience of Chaos, Vulkan was struck by a revelation. All things were interconnected. The orks seemed random but they were not. They were *emergent*. Trial and error always began with wildness and accidental circumstance, but it honed and refined. It evolved.

As the orks had evolved of late – hyper-evolved in the accelerating presence of the Great Beast – so their strategy had evolved. From gargants to hulks, to attack moons, to Ullanor itself – a progression that, once revealed, could be followed back to its base in the most simple of ork constructions.

And the same was true of all their acts.

Learn through action. Trial and error.

The attack moons were not battle stations, or at least not merely battle stations. They were test shots, dry runs sent out into the void as the orks tinkered and improved their gravitic engines.

And once the technology had been proven they needed to find a target. The Great Beast had not struck early, it had struck a bargain. It would avenge the abused spirit of the orks, it would crush the Emperor that had humbled orkdom. On the crescendo of such a victory its power would be unlimited and it would ascend to rule of the galaxy.

And now, Vulkan realised in that instant of feverish thought, they had found Earth. They had located the Throneworld and humanity had proven itself incapable of fighting back.

The attack moon over Earth was a beacon as much as a vanguard. Ullanor, the whole world, was the same thinking writ on a planetary scale – a base of billions of orks. It had been armed and protected like an attack moon. Could it also be moved across star systems like one? If Terra was the target...

There really was no way to stop the Great Beast by any conventional means.

Such power could not be destroyed, only diverted. Feeling the last gasps of breath escaping his body, Vulkan let his thoughts flow again. He reached out into the undulating waaagh, tapping into that warp-born part of himself that had been for every primarch a blessing and a curse. He allowed his primal essence to mix with that of the orks, his Emperor-created body absorbing the surge of energy like a sponge.

He allowed the pure orkishness that had killed so many Librarians to infuse his body. Vulkan felt the Great Beast tense, its thoughts moving to him with tectonic slowness as it realised something was amiss. It tried to pull back the waaagh, to wrest the raw orkish power from the mind of the primarch.

Vulkan only had a moment before he lost the battle, before the power of the orks and the last dregs of his life were both spent.

With failing muscles, he thrust Doomtremor into the face of the Great Beast and detonated the power field generator.

The last of the transports lifted away, a battered Thunderhawk in the livery of the Salamanders. Its original occupants had died in the fighting, determined to fight to the last close to their primarch. Now it carried the Lord Commander, two Chapter Masters and a wounded captain of the Blood Angels. High company in dire circumstances.

Koorland looked down at the dwindling city below from the open ramp, his thoughts at a standstill. His gaze roved over the mounds of dead and the broken ruins where tech-priests and skitarii, tanks and Guardsmen still battled for no reason other than survival. Drop-ships were coming for them, but few would get off Ullanor.

He could have done no more, he was certain of it. Had he done enough? Had he done the right thing? Koorland knew that only history would make that judgement, but he had to believe in the truth of Vulkan's assertion.

'Lord Commander! The temple-gargant!'

Thane's call drew Koorland's attention back to the inner city. A shuddering wave of green power flowed out from the temple-gargant. The floating citadel was listing heavily, its front bastions carving a ruinous path through what little remained of the city centre as it descended. The entire structure writhed with green flames, and at the heart of an inferno of raw energy Koorland thought he saw flickering images of two immense beings, locked together in an embrace of mutual destruction.

The bubbling shockwave crackled out for several kilometres, passing over and through everything. Koorland watched as it overtook the last remnants of Adeptus Mechanicus and Astra Militarum trying to flee the devastation. Tanks and cybernetica were tossed like grains of sand. Roaming ork mobs were taken up in the wave, borne up into the green cloud like flecks of flotsam on an incoming tide.

Stretching nearly a kilometre across, the detonation rapidly slowed and then stopped.

Koorland held his breath for several seconds as the immense green hemisphere wavered, balanced perfectly between expansion and retraction.

Then the field collapsed.

In seconds the implosion raced back to the temple-gargant,

scouring clear everything that had been encompassed in its girth, ripping Gorkogrod down to the foundations and swallowing the pinnacle of the mountain with its ravening energy.

The temple-gargant split asunder, crashing into the scourged ground spouting pillars of green fire and storms of jade lightning, breaking apart into hundreds of hab-block sized chunks, scattering masonry and metal.

Just before the Thunderhawk passed into the cloud cover, Koorland could see the ork armies amassing around the capital, a ring of smoke and darkness several kilometres deep. Millions of orks from across Ullanor, poised just half a day from pouring into Gorkogrod. There was no chance of going back.

'Is it dead?' asked Thane, leaning around the Lord Commander to look at the devastation wrought by the temple-gargant's destruction. 'Did Vulkan kill it?'

'Have faith,' replied Koorland.

EPILOGUE

Terra – outer system

Koorland was in the strategium when the *Alcazar Remem-bered* broke warp back in the Sol System. Transit back to the Terran system had been swift, the warp-roar of the orks momentarily quelled. A few hundred Space Marines had made the journey with him. Perhaps ten times that number from the Astra Militarum, Imperial Navy and Cult Mechanicus had been lifted from the city before the orks had reclaimed it.

Nobody had felt like celebrating a victory.

The strategium was tense. There had been no confirmed contact with Terra. It was impossible to know whether the strike had been in time. Were they simply returning to the ashes of the Throneworld?

Koorland did not think so. When the time came, the Great Beast would have led the attack. He had learnt as much from the actions of Vulkan.

'Any transmissions?' he asked Kale.

The shipmaster shook his head.

Thane was with him. So many were not. The Exemplar remarked as much.

'They will be honoured, each one,' the last of the Imperial Fists replied. 'They were all heroes of the Imperium, from the mighty such as Odaenathus who fell against the Great Beast itself to the first Guardsman who died in the planetstrike. And Vulkan, his passing shall be mourned for millennia. Without each and every one of them we could not have prevailed. It is our duty that their deaths are not squandered. We have shown what we can do, when united in ambition, and led with purpose. The orks have shown us how broken we had become. The wounds are still raw but it is not too late to tend them, brother.'

'Lord Commander, I am detecting a powerful transmission,' one of the deck officers announced. 'Source origin is Terran orbit. Looped signal. All major channels. I'm going to–'

The officer stood up straight, face ashen, headset falling to his console. His terrified gaze moved to Koorland while his mouth continued to work silently, unable to form the words needed.

'On audible,' the Lord Commander snapped. The officer's trembling finger activated a rune.

The speakers crackled into life, and from them issued a deep, grating voice, slowly repeating the same words.

'I am Slaughter! I am Slaughter! I am Slaughter! I am Slaughter!'

ABOUT THE AUTHOR

Gav Thorpe is the author of the Horus Heresy novel *Deliverance Lost*, as well as the novellas *Corax: Soulforge, Ravenlord* and *The Lion*, which formed part of the *New York Times* bestselling collection *The Primarchs*. He is particularly well-known for his Dark Angels stories, including the Legacy of Caliban series. His Warhammer 40,000 repertoire further includes the Path of the Eldar series, the Horus Heresy audio dramas *Raven's Flight, Honour to the Dead* and *Raptor*, and a multiplicity of short stories. For Warhammer, Gav has penned the End Times novel *The Curse of Khaine*, the Time of Legends trilogy, *The Sundering*, and much more besides. He lives and works in Nottingham.

The Beast Arises continues in Book 9

Watchers in Death

by David Annandale

August 2016

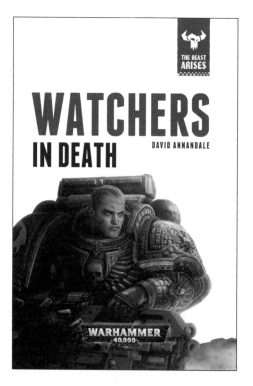

Available from
blacklibrary.com and

Extract from

Watchers in Death

by David Annandale

'The decryption is complete,' Segorine said.

'Thank you,' said Koorland. He and Thane followed her down the chapel aisle to where the other tech-priests waited. Behind the altar, a large pict screen pulsed with snow.

'Faith,' said Eternity.

Koorland waited.

Segorine snaked out a limb to a control panel built into the altar. She depressed a dial, and the screen came to life. The images flickered and jumped. The muzzles of beam weapons flared everything to white. Explosions broke up the picture.

But the worst distortion came from unleashed psychic energy. Koorland saw the Black Templars at bay, fighting hard against the ork horde. He saw the greenskin psyker, its power ferocious, seeming to destroy the reality along with the images. He saw the Black Templars pray as they fought. The sound was a riot of distortion, a grating rhythm barely recognisable as gunfire. Breaking through in fragments were deep, sonorous chants, magnified by vox-casters. The voices of faith travelled across destruction and time to frame their moment of victory.

For a moment, the sound cleared altogether. The yowls of the orks and the concussions of the guns vanished. There was only the stern, martial prayer of the Black Templars. The energy flares of the witch stuttered, then spread out as if they had hit a wall. They curled away from the Space Marines. Koorland leaned forward, astonished. Arcing waves of power slammed back into the greenskin psyker. The beast's mouth opened wide, its face contorted, and still there was only the sound of the chanting. The ork's eyes burst. It exploded into flame. The energy flashed across the frame of the feed, utterly uncontrolled, blasting every ork to ash. The energy storm swallowed up the chanting. The chapel filled with a shattering feedback shriek, and the visual feed disintegrated.

The screen returned to snow, then went black.

'The visible energy,' Thane said slowly. 'I didn't see it come from the Black Templars.'

'No,' Koorland agreed. 'It was all from the ork psyker.' To the tech-priests he said, 'Will you play that back again? Slowly.'

They watched. At the end, Thane said, 'Are the orks and their witches linked?'

'In some way, they must be,' said Koorland. He could see no other interpretation. The psyker's death had triggered the immolation of the horde.

'So if we can target their psykers...'

'A possible weakness, yes.' Koorland turned to Eternity.

'That was not the work of a single warrior, was it?' Certainly not a Librarian. The Black Templars allowed no psykers within the ranks of their battle-brethren.

'That was the faith of all my brothers present in that battle,' said Eternity. 'A collective strength.'

'Against a single ork witch,' said Thane.

'Its fall destroyed its entire force,' Eternity pointed out.

'Yes,' said Koorland. 'Yes it did.'

If only we'd known. The words came to him unbidden, a canker on his soul. He tried to push them away. He tried to tell himself the Imperial tactics on Ullanor would not have been altered, but his grief would permit no such comfort.

If only they had known. They would have fought differently. They would have made a greater priority of finding and taking out the ork psykers. They would have targeted the source of greenskin strength and turned it into a weakness.

He thought of Vulkan. The primarch had wished for the aid of the Sisters of Silence. He had recognised the need for a strong counter to the psykers.

He must have known, Koorland thought. He tried again to tell himself, *We would not have fought any differently.*

He knew that wasn't true.

Neither were many things, he thought, that he had been telling himself of late. He had worked hard to maintain an illusion of self that made it possible for him to carry the responsibility he had shouldered. It made it possible for him to lead. But he had led nowhere except to disaster. He had nothing but contempt for the High Lords. At this moment, though, he was not sure how he was any different from them.

He forced himself to focus on the moment. 'We may not see the key to the weakness in this data,' he said. 'But it *is* a weakness, and we *will* exploit it.'

An hour later, Koorland was still thinking about difference, his mind chasing itself in a toxic spiral. He walked alone on the ramparts of Daylight Wall, looking up into the night of Terra. There was a strong wind, and the sulphurous clouds over the Imperial Palace roiled, broke and reformed. In the gaps of their anger, the light of two moons reached down. Luna was a narrow, waning crescent. The reflected glow of the ork attack moon was paler, colder and more baleful. That threat was over, or at least contained. The orks were gone, the moon blockaded. But it was still a presence in the Terran sky, an insult and a wound to the heart of the Imperium. No enemy, even defeated, should ever have come so close.

He pictured another moon. He pictured several. Next time, the orks might not hold back from deploying their gravity weapons against Terra. They might no longer have any interest in conquest. They had been bloodied on Ullanor. Their vengeance might well take the form of total destruction.

And even if the moon was dead, it was not silent. It roared. *I AM SLAUGHTER. I AM SLAUGHTER. I AM SLAUGHTER.* The broadcast was ceaseless. It was gigantic. It would take nothing for Koorland to open a vox-channel and hear it.

He chose not to, but the reality of the shout was another poison in the toxic silence. The words of the Beast hammered at Terra, breaking down the spirit of citizens. The roar mocked the sacrifices on Ullanor. It declared the futility of every Imperial endeavour to stop the orks. Every great quest, every journey, every challenge, every hard-won battle and shard of hope – they all meant nothing. What did they have to show for Caldera, for Ullanor? Even their victory against the moon was turned into mockery.

Koorland grieved, and so did all the world. He did not know fear, but he knew its cancer possessed every mortal soul on Terra.

The battlements of Daylight Wall were built upon many terraces. Turrets and cannon emplacements on multiple levels faced the east, so many it seemed they should be able to kill the rising sun if it dared to challenge the Emperor. Koorland walked along the top. He took up a position between the crenellations and looked down at the bristling strength below him. Not long ago, this perspective would have renewed his sense of duty and of purpose. Now he observed the defences and thought: Not enough.

The guns were insufficient.

So was he.

The approaching footsteps were quiet, more from a desire not to disturb than not to be heard. Koorland turned to the right. Drakan Vangorich, Grand Master of the Officio Assassinorum, walked down the wide avenue of the wall toward him. There was enough room between the battlements for a Baneblade to pass, and the Assassin was a tiny figure in the night. On either side, the relief sculptures of the crenellations celebrated Imperial might. Heroic figures cut down their foes with sword and gun. Koorland's eyes went back and forth from the brutal strength of the stone to the wiry Grand Master. In the contrast, he felt a glimmer of inspiration. It passed before he could discern its shape.

Vangorich nodded to Koorland as he drew near. 'A home-coming?' he asked.

'No,' said Koorland. 'Daylight Wall Company is gone. And my duty is no longer named by a single battlement.'

'It was never limited to that, though.'

'No, it wasn't.' Koorland sighed. 'But there was great order in that naming. Symbols have powerful meaning.'

'As does their loss,' Vangorich said quietly.

'Yes.' The annihilation of Daylight Wall Company was of little importance next to the loss of a Chapter. And what was even that compared to the death of a primarch?

'I've seen the recording,' Vangorich said.

'For all the good it does us now.'

Vangorich gave him a sharp look. 'Defeatism doesn't suit you, Lord Commander Koorland.'

'Neither does naiveté,' Koorland said.

Vangorich was quiet for a moment. Then he said, 'It isn't that long since we last spoke on this wall.'

'It isn't, and I don't come here seeking to have my morale boosted by you.'

'It would be an odd thing to do, given my particular duty.'
Koorland grunted.

'I hope, though,' Vangorich went on, 'that you will listen to counsel.'

'I know what you would have to say about being a symbol.'

'And you would deny its truth.'

'I would deny my fitness to serve as that symbol.'

'Would you deny your duty to do so?'

'You know I would not,' Koorland growled. Duty and fitness were very different things, and he resented Vangorich's blurring of the two.

'No,' the Grand Master said. 'You have never turned from your duty. You have always done it. You did it on Ullanor too.'

'To no end.'

'And who would have been better suited? Who should have led instead?'

Koorland didn't answer. He might have said, 'Vulkan.' Yet the primarch had left much of the control of the campaign in his hands.

'Vulkan left much of the campaign in your hands, didn't he?' Vangorich said.

'He did.'

'Was he wrong? Did he err?'

Koorland looked down at the Grand Master and glared. Again he said nothing. He could not bring himself to say aloud that Vulkan had been mistaken. He would not question the final decisions of the last primarch.

'I'll take your silence as a *no*,' Vangorich said.

'You're playing a game with words,' said Koorland. 'It isn't amusing, and it isn't useful.'

'You're right,' Vangorich said, his tone suddenly sharp. 'There would be nothing useful in a game. The High Lords have proven this many times over, and as far as I can tell, they're very much intent on proving it yet again. I am not playing at anything. What we need right now is clarity, don't you agree?'

'I do.' He grimaced. 'We could have used the clarity of Magneric's information on Ullanor.'

'Exactly. Obfuscation, illusion, denial, ignorance, they have brought us disaster.'

So has everything else, Koorland thought. He said, 'Your point, when you reach it, will have to be an impressive one, Drakan.'

'Did Vulkan speak to you before the end?'

'He did.'

'And?'

Koorland took a deep breath. He let it out with a shudder, as if it could expel the burdens and memories that had built up like a toxic cloud inside his chest. 'He ordered me to carry on.'

'That was all?'

'He called me Lord Commander. He said I was the Imperial Fists.'

'And you would dismiss those words?'

Koorland shook his head. 'It isn't that simple.'

'I see nothing simple in what I am suggesting. I see that you have a great burden to carry, one that is enormously complex. It is yours, however. You shouldered it after Ardamantua. You have carried it since. Vulkan reaffirmed your duty to carry on. It is your burden, because you have the strength for it. The primarch saw you are the leader we need now. So do all your brothers. Across the Chapters.'

Koorland narrowed his gaze in disbelief.

'Your doubt has no place here, Lord Commander,' Vangorich said. 'Unless your information is more complete than mine. Has there been a challenge to your leadership? Has one of the surviving Space Wolves stepped forward to declare himself the alpha of the campaign?'

'No,' said Koorland. 'And I would thank you to refer to those Space Marines with greater respect. They have sacrificed much.'

'All have,' Vangorich said softly. 'And the mission was a disaster. Yet there has been no challenge. There is a reason for that. They see what Vulkan saw. They await your orders.'

'My orders.'

'I assume you aren't going to wait for the orks to attack first.'

Koorland felt the corners of his lips pull back. After a moment he realised something like a smile, cold and hard and hungry, had appeared on his face. 'You're very good at what you do,' he told Vangorich.

'I have to be.'

Koorland studied the Grand Master. 'Perhaps we should learn from you,' he said. As he spoke, the feeling of inspiration returned. It was stronger now. Closer to being something he could articulate.

'What do you think I could teach you?'

'Precision,' Koorland said. The idea had almost formed. 'You rely on few to do work that affects many.'

'Precision is the correct word,' said Vangorich. 'What is necessary is not overwhelming force. What is needed is the right weapon and the right target.'

'Which we have lacked,' Koorland muttered.

'The weapon or the target?'

'Both. We thought we had found the Beast on Ullanor. Vulkan gave his life to slay it. And now...' He pointed at the attack moon.

I AM SLAUGHTER, said the silence.

Koorland felt the words without hearing them. He saw Vangorich wince, and knew the Grand Master felt them too.

'The Beast survived?' Vangorich asked.

'No. It can't have. Yet something with its voice lives on. And that palace on Ullanor...'

'Yes,' said Vangorich. He understood. The horror was not lost on him.

'They are creating an empire,' Koorland said. 'They plan to build it on the ashes of our own.'

Vangorich nodded. 'The ambassadors,' he said.

'What about them?'

'More evidence of the construction of an empire. The greenskins are evolving the classes that will be needed for an empire to function.' He nodded to himself again. 'So,' he said. 'No matter what died on Ullanor, the force of the Beast lives on. We have to consider what this means for our strategy.'

'Our attack was too blunt. We were not a surprise. The orks knew what was coming, and prepared for us.'

'What do you conclude, then?'

'We need to keep looking for the Beast. In whatever form the guiding power of the orks exists, let us call it that. If we destroy it...'

'The ork empire will fall,' Vangorich finished. 'A decapitation. You need to commit yourself to that, Lord Commander.'

'We are. We were. We have to change our methods, though. If we come at the orks again as we did, even if we could assemble such a force again, they will win again. They outnumber us, and they outgun us.' The last admission was the hardest. The entire history of the Imperium's fight against the orks had involved the superiority of humanity's technology against the orks' vast tide of savagery. Recognising that the orks' technology had outstripped the Imperium's was a perpetually re-opened wound. It had been the most basic fact of the war since Ardamantua, but speaking the words aloud sounded perilously close to capitulation. Not to face that reality, would lead to true defeat. 'We have to hit them another way.'

The inspiration that had teased the edge of his consciousness burst upon him. It had the clarity of revelation. He had known the same certainty when he had called for a unified command of the Imperial Fists Successor Chapters. Then, as now, the epiphany had come in the wake of devastating loss. Then, as now, he saw his course of action allowed for no doubt. He might question his own worthiness. He knew he would. But the path to follow shone before him.

He did not look at what he must do as cause for hope. It might yet fail. It was, instead, the thing that must be done. It was the one move left that the orks might not be able to counter.

'Sometimes,' Vangorich said, unknowingly giving voice to Koorland's revelation, 'a single knife can be more effective than a broadsword.'

'Yes,' Koorland said. '*Yes.* As your Officio has shown throughout its history. I'm interested in your tactics, Drakan. We need to learn from them. *That* is the counsel I would welcome from you.'

'The Adeptus Astartes are not assassins,' Vangorich said. He sounded cautious. 'There are paths we must be careful not to take, if we do not want to repeat mistakes a thousand years old.'

'We aren't assassins,' Koorland agreed. He respected Vangorich, but more, the Grand Master was the one member of the High Council for whom he felt anything even remotely approaching trust. He respected Veritus and Wienand, but he did not trust either. They were too immersed in the political machinations of the Ordos. Veritus, in particular, he did not trust to act as the needs of the immediate crisis dictated. But now, as Vangorich spoke, Koorland saw the politician emerge in him. His caution was genuine. Even so, Koorland sensed an instinctive territorial defence.

Vangorich did not have to worry. Koorland had no interest in assassination. Decapitation was still the goal. And now he could imagine a new means to that end.

'I don't want to know about your organisation, your weapons or your specific tactics,' Koorland said. 'I want to hear about the broader strategy. Your philosophy of war.'

Vangorich gave him a half-smile. 'You think the Officio Assassinorum goes to war?'

'Of course it does, even if it might use a different name.'

Vangorich parted his hands, conceding the point. 'Go on,' he said.

'Tell me about the knife, and how it strikes.'